"Are you scared?"

The delicious thrum of the motor against her inner thighs and the challenge in his voice made her close the gap between their bodies.

"Not a bit," she assured him, even though her heart was in the pit of her stomach.

"Good, because I would never hurt you."

At his words, her heart melted. His body heat radiated through his clothes, and his masculinity draped around him, heavy and comfortable. She sensed she could snuggle up in his arms, fall asleep and not have to worry about a thing.

How she wished she could sweep everything that kept her up at night away from her mind, replace it all with a man who would sweep her right off her feet. She wasn't looking for it, but she'd never stopped hoping for a second chance at love.

She inched even closer, until… She could feel his abdomen tense up.

Oh, my, she thought with a lick of h̶

His muscles were so d̶
could climb a mou̶
wouldn't fall.

"That's better," he sa̶ ̶ ̶ ̶ ̶ ̶on as
tight as you'd like. I ̶

She nodded, inhaling the scent of his leather jacket. She had visions of him wearing it and nothing else.

Dear Reader,

At first glance, Trent Waterson, a real estate mogul, and Sonya Young, a former professional ballerina, are an unlikely couple. They differ in family background and career choices. But they can agree on one thing: the moment they meet, they both feel a tug in their hearts toward one another, even if they don't want to admit it.

Winning Her Forever is set in the fictional idyllic beach town of Bay Point, California. Stay tuned for *Winning Her Holiday Love*, my first holiday-themed novel. I appreciate your continued support.

Sincerely,

Harmony Evans

www.HarmonyEvans.com

WINNING
Her
FOREVER

Harmony Evans

H HARLEQUIN® KIMANI™ ROMANCE

Recycling programs
for this product may
not exist in your area.

ISBN-13: 978-1-335-21685-4

Winning Her Forever

HARLEQUIN®
™ www.Harlequin.com

Printed in U.S.A.

Harmony Evans received the 2013 Romance Slam Jam Emma Award for Debut Author of the Year. Her first book, *Lesson in Romance*, garnered two RT Reviewers' Choice Best Book Award nominations in 2012. She currently resides in New York City. Visit her at www.harmonyevans.com.

Books by Harmony Evans

Harlequin Kimani Romance

Lesson in Romance
Stealing Kisses
Loving Laney
When Morning Comes
Winning Her Love
Winning the Doctor
Winning Her Heart
Winning Her Forever

Visit the Author Page
at Harlequin.com for more titles.

Chapter 1

Sonya headed toward the classroom listed on her registration form. The hall was quiet and empty, too quiet, in fact, and she wondered if she was in the right building. Her nerves crackled in anticipation of the evening ahead.

It felt surreal, and a little scary, to be back on a college campus, but it was just one of the many steps she'd taken to create a new life for herself.

When she reached the room, she tried the door, but it was locked. There was no sign posted on the glass, and no one inside. She leaned against the wall and dug out her phone, hoping for a last-minute email informing her that the room had been changed.

While she was navigating to the application, the device shut off.

She recalled reading in her information packet that any class changes would be posted in the registrar's office. She dropped her phone back into her canvas tote bag, dug around and groaned. In addition to forgetting to charge her phone, she had left the hard copy of the campus map at home.

Back outside, Sonya zipped up her lime-green rain jacket, ducked under her umbrella and glanced around. The Bay Point Community College campus was larger than she'd expected, and was bustling with students going to and from evening classes. There was a coffee shop near the parking lot. Maybe one of the baristas could give her directions to the registrar's office.

She hurried toward it, weaving around puddles and dodging other students. By the time she arrived, the rain was slanting sideways. Afraid of getting her newly permed hair wet, she opened the door and stepped over the threshold into the coffee shop.

"Dumb thing," she muttered as she struggled to retract her large pink-and-brown-polka-dotted umbrella.

"Hey, watch out!"

A man's voice, bass-low and heavy with concern, washed over her.

She shook her head to reorient herself, pressed

the button a few times, and after a long agonizing moment, the umbrella finally closed.

As she lowered it, her breath caught in her throat at the gorgeous man that stood in front of her, revealed like a game-show grand prize. His grim expression and now-empty paper cup in his hand led her to believe that all was not right in his world.

Her eyes widened at the large stain snow-flaking across the middle of his light blue T-shirt, no doubt caused by her.

"I'm sorry. My umbrella jammed. Are you hurt?"

The man furrowed his brow. "I'm fine."

But she barely heard his words. Her thoughts were consumed with the desire to allow her fingers the freedom to graze the fabric plastered to his flat abdomen.

As a former ballet dancer, she had a deep appreciation for the beauty and majesty of the human body, especially the male form. And this particular man was ripe for tactile exploration. Faded dark blue jeans, paint-spattered construction boots and rampant tattoos over dark honey arms were all reasons for an extended pause.

He is hot, hot, hot.

He waved a hand in front of her face. "Are you okay?"

She jerked her chin up and her cheeks bloomed with heat at the amusement in his eyes. "Y-yes. I was just worried that you got burned."

"No. Lucky for me, it was just very cold iced coffee."

As she exhaled in relief, he smiled, displaying perfect white teeth.

"Lucky for you, I like surprises."

Before she could think of a response, he pointed down at the floor between them. "Watch out."

With her eyes still on his, she stepped back from the spreading liquid, and bumped into a pregnant woman trying to exit.

Sonya apologized and stepped closer to the man so the woman could pass. She was so embarrassed she almost joined the cluster of ice cubes melting on the floor.

"Do you come with a warning?"

"No. Do you?" she challenged.

He raised a brow, but it was hard to tell if he was irked or intrigued.

"Yeah, it's called never argue with a pretty lady."

Her mouth dropped open and another buzz of unexpected heat rose in her cheeks. The grin on his face seemed sincere, and that was the problem.

She didn't feel pretty at that moment, just cold and lost, and she had no time for flirtation.

He seemed not to notice her response, and instead directed her with his hand, around the puddle and deeper into the store.

He touched her elbow. "Let's move out of everyone's way, shall we?"

Even through her rain jacket, a shock wave of pleasure went zinging through her veins like a ball in a pinball machine. Though she'd never seen this man before, his gentle guidance felt protective. But just as quickly, he released her. She watched as he slid a navy blue backpack off his shoulders and set it down on the counter. His large hands looked as if they could level three men with one punch, or caress her body with ease.

The loss of his brief touch left her feeling unsettled. He pulled out the chair next to his, and the sound of metal scraping against the tile floor brought her out of her daze.

Sonya let out a breath and joined him, but kept her messenger bag on.

Rain pelted the window in a torrential, thunderous downpour. The noise level in the shop elevated as people hurried inside to escape the weather.

"Looks like we're stuck here together for a while."

She worried her lip, knowing that further delays would not help the fact that she didn't know the location of her class.

"Could my night get any worse?"

His laugh was deep and genuine. "That's the first time I've ever heard that comment from a woman."

Sonya frowned at his audacious statement, which smacked of the type of egoism she'd grown up with in her own family and had eventually escaped.

She took a step closer to him, to the outer fringes

of his personal space. His rough-and-ready aura felt familiar, almost cozy. Every fiber of her being wanted to step back again, but she held her ground.

"I'm sorry I made you spill your coffee, but I've had a really rough day, and I don't need the sarcasm."

She ignored his sardonic grin, dug into her messenger bag and dropped a crumpled five-dollar bill on the counter.

"I hope this covers your loss."

He looked over at it, then back at her and his smile faded.

"Put your money away. I don't need it."

His sharp tone was like a switch, instantly flooding her face with embarrassment. She had the sense he was offended she'd even made the gesture, and now she wished she hadn't.

She steadied her voice. "Are you sure?"

"Yeah."

She cupped her palm over the bill and stuffed it back into her bag.

His eyes, a deep chocolate-brown flecked with green, sought hers. Though he was a stranger, she couldn't help but be drawn into the sphere of his intense gaze.

"I could wash your shirt for you," she offered, only half kidding.

"Then I'd have to take it off," he said grimly.

That's the whole point, she thought.

Her lips began to tilt out a smile, but she forced

them back into a straight line. He raised his brow, as if he'd read her mind, and a searing flame of attraction lit up her insides.

"Actually, I'm more worried about you. Are you sure you're all right? You do look a little frazzled."

She reached up and patted her shoulder-length curls. "You mean, frizzled, right?"

His laughter made her glow in all the places it shouldn't. It felt honest and real and warm, not patronizing or unappreciative. She had a feeling that he was the kind of guy who wouldn't care if she showed up at his door sans makeup or clothes.

"As a matter of fact, I'm lost," she admitted.

"Oh? Are you a new student here?"

"Trying to be. I went to the assigned classroom on my registration form, but no one was there and no sign was posted. There has to be some mistake."

"Maybe it was canceled?"

She frowned. "I hope not. Anyway, can you point me in the direction of the registrar's office?"

The rain had slowed, so they ventured outside. He put his umbrella up and motioned her to join him.

He was broad-shouldered, and she barely fit under the umbrella as she sidled up next to him. He smelled faintly of sawdust and spice, making her think of crisp autumn leaves and a crackling, roaring fire. The barest hint of a dark shadow, apparent on his strong angled jaw, suited him.

He switched the handle of the umbrella to his

other hand and pointed the way. His knuckles appeared slightly rough and her eyes traced the sinew of his muscled forearm up to where the fabric of his T-shirt stretched to accommodate his massive bicep. He emanated the kind of outward strength that a man couldn't get from hours at the gym or behind a desk, but only from years of hard work.

As he gave her directions, his voice rumbled through her ears on a wave of authority and could probably make the most mundane topics sound exciting. If only she could listen to him, over and over again.

If only his arm was draped around her shoulders, tugging her closer and closer.

If only...

She sucked in a breath and woke up from her momentary daydream with a pleasurable tug in her loins and the knowledge that he was the cause.

"Thanks for the info." She ducked out from under his umbrella and opened up her own. "I better get going, so I'm not late."

His gaze lingered, agitating the butterflies already swirling in her stomach.

"See you again soon?"

Sonya shrugged, mumbled another thanks and left in a hurry, before she forgot the directions to the office.

See him again?

Not a chance.

She didn't really have a type, but if she did, a T-shirt, tattoos and old work boots kind of guy wasn't high on her list, even though he looked divine in all three. Yet a part of her longed to stay and sweep the edge of her knuckles gently against the planes of his bristled jaw, just to see if this rough-hewn man would shiver under her touch.

Why didn't I get her name?

Trent gripped his umbrella and watched the beautiful woman hurry away. She seemed to glide along the slick wet pavement, lending a sense of elegance to her black old-school ankle-high sneakers.

Dark blue skinny jeans molded her slender hips and long legs. Her long neck reminded him of a swan, one of his favorite animals. When he was in college, he'd taken a zoology class and learned that swans mated for life. He had been fascinated with them ever since.

The green rain slicker zipped up high hid everything else, but he had a feeling he would like what was underneath, just as she seemed to like him.

His parents, whom he loved dearly, would soon celebrate their twenty-fifth wedding anniversary. Despite their insistence that he settle down, he wasn't in a rush. Someday, he hoped to find a woman to love and protect for a lifetime. If the right woman stepped into his life, he wasn't sure if he could make the leap from bachelor to husband. It was the permanence of marriage and the statistics of divorce that frightened him more than the fear of being alone for the rest of his life.

Like a cold engine, relationships were tricky to start, and even harder to keep going. Up until now, he hadn't had the patience or the time.

But this woman, she was different.

The luminous glow of her caramel toned face would no doubt stay in his mind for a long time. The undercurrent of seriousness in her demeanor was equally attractive, although he had no idea the reason behind it.

The offer to launder his shirt had surprised and delighted him. This woman was a giver, not a taker. He could feel it.

The sense that he'd lost something he didn't know he could have had grew stronger as she disappeared into the college's nondescript administrative building.

He always made the first move, but this time he hadn't. Big mistake.

He retracted his umbrella and looped his arms through the straps of his backpack. If he didn't hurry, he'd be late, too. His heavy boots slapped against the cement as he walked toward Reed Hall, inhaling the rain-fresh air into his lungs.

He pinched the bottom of his T-shirt, wicking it away from his skin. He needed to change the thing before doing anything else.

When he got to the building, he ducked into a nearby men's room and looked in the mirror. The shirt wasn't the problem. He always kept an extra one or two in his backpack because getting dirty was just part of his job. He was a simple man, who liked to be prepared for anything.

When he got thirsty, he drank. On a hot day, he'd been known to unscrew the cover of his five-gallon water jug and pour the whole thing over his head. That was why he always carried two in his pickup truck.

When he got hungry, he ate. He eschewed all types of red meat, in favor of fish and vegetables.

And when he got lonely, his contact list was full of women to choose from. Sometimes, he'd scroll for one. Make a hit. Roll over and say goodbye.

Lately, he wanted more substance in his relationships. Not an immediate yes, and certainly not a please yes. He loved the thrill and the challenge of the chase, because it was something he could control and build upon.

Day by day, night by night, fight by fight.

That exquisite internal yearning. Not knowing if he was on a woman's mind, even though she occupied his, or whether she truly wanted to be with him and him alone.

He glanced into the mirror, and could see the need and loneliness in his eyes. The wet shirt wasn't the problem. The beautiful mystery lady was the real shock to his system, and he wanted more of her, and he had no idea how to find her. Maybe he should have been a detective rather than a builder.

Trent changed into a dry shirt and washed his hands, ignoring the sudden cramp in his stomach. Being nervous did not mesh with his normal level-headed demeanor.

He liked to build things and tear them down. As part owner of Waterson Builders, one of the largest construction and real-estate companies in Bay Point, he got paid to do both. Working his craft was easy, but trying to teach it? He was still trying to figure out why he'd agreed to stimulate adult female minds with the basics of home repair.

His older brother, Steve, the other half of the family company, was originally scheduled to teach the class. Trent smirked in the mirror, recalling how Steve had called him last night and begged him to take his place. His brother might be a pain in the ass, but he was no fool. The only reason he had asked Trent to step in was because he knew that he would say yes.

He shook his head and though he was tired of bailing his brother out, family was numero uno. His parents had drilled that into his head ever since he was a kid.

Steve, who was quite selfish and preferred to be in the spotlight, hadn't gotten the message. Unlike his brother, Trent would rather be in the bucket seat of a dozer.

He pushed his family issues to another corner of his mind and opened the door to the woodworking shop. The chatter in the room immediately stopped, and when he saw who was in the first row of worktables, so did his heart.

Chapter 2

"Welcome to Everyday Repairs for Women. I'm Trent Waterson, your instructor."

Sonya's mouth dropped open and she almost did a double take as he thumped his backpack down onto the old wooden desk at the front of the room.

The man from the coffee shop was her teacher?

He'd changed into a plain white cotton shirt. Though it appeared worn, on him it looked as though it had cost hundreds of dollars.

He scanned the room with a friendly expression on his face. There was no outward indication that he recognized her. Her heart sank with disappointment. They'd only met fifteen minutes earlier. While she didn't expect him to jump up and say hallelujah, was she that forgettable?

"If you've come here to learn how to fix things, you're in the right place," he continued, palms flattened on the desk. "Though I must warn you, this class will probably not be as exciting as some of the home-improvement shows you may have seen on television, but I do promise you'll have fun."

Sonya detected a hint of a tremor in his authoritative voice, and she looked around the room, wondering if anyone else had heard it, too.

The faces of her classmates were frozen in rapt attention, hanging on the edge of his next word, and she held back a grin. Mr. Waterson must have been the reason for the long waitlist. Lucky for her, a spot had opened up.

Turning her attention to the front of the room, she found the possibility that he might be even a tiny bit nervous very intriguing. It made him as real as the muscles she'd felt on his abdomen, and the spark of attraction she'd felt between them.

Violet, a diminutive light-skinned woman with purple tinged strands in her close-cropped jet-black hair nudged her arm.

"Didn't I tell you he was gorgeous?" she whispered low.

Before Sonya could nod in agreement, another poke followed, this time harder.

"Too bad he's a heartbreaker."

"Ow, girl!" Sonya exclaimed and jerked her body away so fast that she almost fell off the old iron bar stool. Violet's comment had piqued her interest about the man, but she wasn't keen on believing gossip. If she ever got the chance, she would ask him outright.

Trent raised a brow at their antics. His gaze laser-focused on her and by the sudden flutter in her heart, there was no question now that he recognized her.

"Ladies, is there a problem?"

"Are you trying to get us into trouble?" Sonya hissed out of the corner of her mouth.

She wanted to slide like a cartoon character straight to the woodshop floor with embarrassment.

"No worries," Violet whispered back. "I got you, girl. Let me handle this."

Violet raised her hand. "What happened?"

"The other Mr. Waterson couldn't make it, so I guess you're stuck with me." He looked about the room. "Is that okay?"

While heads were nodding, Sonya inched her hand up as he zipped his backpack open.

"Just for tonight?"

"Just for forever," he replied with a grin that felt like it was meant only for her. "Or rather the twelve weeks that this class will be in session."

Forever.

What would that feel like, look like, with a guy as handsome as Trent Waterson? The only thing missing was a tool belt around his waist. When he dug around in his bag, brought one out and hooked it on, it was like an invisible genie had heard her secret wish.

Sporadic applause broke out and Sonya lowered her hand. Smiles widened from the windows to the chalkboard, as if he'd just presented them all with sparkling diamond rings.

He'll cause mass depression if he ever calls in sick.

Sonya glanced around the workshop filled with scary-looking equipment. Her nose twitched, detecting the scent of sawdust and burnt tires. The white-washed cinderblock walls were smudged in places with something she hoped was dirt. This wasn't the ideal place for romantic daydreams.

Her eyes shifted to the front of the room where Trent was taking a sheaf of papers out of his backpack.

"Let me tell you a little bit about myself. My brother and I are joint owners of a local construction and real-estate company, and if you mention his name in my classroom, you'll earn yourself an instant F."

He sounded as if he was kidding, but Sonya wanted to be sure, so she raised her hand again.

"Mr. Waterson. This is a non-credit course and there are no grades. It is pass or fail."

He consulted a folder on the desk and frowned. "You're right. I was mistaken. You'll simply fail."

The class fell silent, and though his tone was still lighthearted, she sensed that the rivalry between Trent and his brother was not.

Sonya felt her nerves start to percolate as Trent moved around the room, handing out the syllabus to every woman.

Her anxiety seemed to increase as he got closer and closer to her. When he reached her worktable, he gave one syllabus to Violet and then turned to Sonya.

"Glad you finally found your way."

His fingertips brushed against hers, and their slight roughness titillated her senses again. Her insides whirled, still in shock that she was even in the same room with him so soon. Their encounter had been brief, but he'd made a lasting impression on her.

As he walked away, she felt dizzy and clasped one hand on the corner of the wooden table to keep from swooning.

Violet leaned over and whispered, "You know him?"

Sonya heard a note of concern in Violet's tone, which both intrigued and touched her. Having just moved back into town after many years away, she needed a friend, one that cared, but hopefully wasn't too nosy.

"No, not really," she responded in a low tone. "I just saw him around on campus."

Back at the front of the room, Trent placed his massive hands, palms down, on the table.

"Now that I've told you a little bit about me, I want to hear about you. Let's start at the front," he said, pointing at her.

Sonya smiled inwardly at the chorus of groans among the women, heartened that she wasn't the only one who hated to talk in front of a group of strangers. Still, she was tickled that he'd chosen her to go first.

"I'm Sonya Young and I grew up in Bay Point. I just moved back about three months ago. I'm a former dancer with the San Francisco Ballet. I'm in the process of opening up a dance studio at the corner of Seascape Drive, right across from the beach."

She exhaled slowly and hoped the confidence in her voice didn't sound as forced as it felt inside.

One of the women exclaimed, "Wonderful. My daughter has always wanted to take ballet. Will you have lessons for children?"

Sonya cleared her throat. Though she loved to dance, the ending of her career was still too new, and too raw. She had plenty of savings, so there was no need to rush the opening of the studio. She was also still questioning her decision and needed time to make sure it was right.

"Children and adults. I'm not sure when I'll be opening. I'm working on launching my studio website, so there will be more details soon."

If ever, she told herself.

"Oh, it's unfortunate that's it's not open right now," the woman responded.

"Is that the storefront that's had the Grand Opening Soon sign in the window for over a month?" asked another woman in the back of the room.

Sonya shifted in her stool and tossed a glance over her shoulder.

"Yes. I plan on opening soon. There's a lot to do." The list of tasks, like design and decorating, marketing and advertising left her with knots in her stomach most days. It was so overwhelming that she continually procrastinated on most, or left others half-completed.

Sonya blamed her own fears as the primary reason for the delay. Making the leap from a career in the arts to opening a small business was scary, but she was determined to be successful.

At least now she'd be in control of her own destiny.

"Hurry up, honey, the butts and thighs of Bay Point need you," Violet chirped.

The room erupted in laughter and there were nods of agreement among the women.

"Hey, I recognize your last name," a third woman piped up. "Your father owned a jewelry store, didn't he?"

Sonya's heart sank at the mention of her dad, who'd owned his store in downtown Bay Point for over twenty-five years. It had been a bone of contention between them ever since she was a little girl.

Before she could interject, the woman continued to rain down comments.

"One day it was open, the next day it wasn't. Odd."

Sonya ignored the opportunity for an explanation. She felt a tinge of sadness, realizing that anybody who paid attention to the local gossip hounds knew that he'd lost the store due to his gambling debts.

But more than that, she was deeply ashamed of her father. Now that she was back, she realized that her negative feelings still loomed. In the past, she'd been able to work out her frustrations on the stage, but that was no longer an option. If she didn't deal with them, she wouldn't be able to move past the pain.

Trent clapped his hands and adjusted his tool belt, drawing all eyes back to the front of the room. Sonya could have kissed him. The only time she liked being the center of attention was when she was on stage.

Every now and then, as each woman introduced herself, Sonya stole glances at Trent. He listened patiently, his arms crossed loosely on his chest, as if he had all the time in the world. When the round-robin was complete, he moved around his worktable.

"Ladies, there are two things you need to be successful in this class. Number one, there's the quick way to do things and there's the right way to do things. The latter is always the best and safest choice. Number two, there's a lot of dangerous equipment in this room, and I don't want anyone touching it without permission."

He leaned against the edge of the worktable, which must have been bolted to the floor because it didn't budge. Beneath his jeans, she imagined tightly muscled thighs and calves. His powerful body radiated strength, drawing her forward in her seat, as if she couldn't get enough of his words. In truth, she was enjoying the unobstructed view of him.

"During this class, you're going to work on a large project and a small project," he continued. "The large project could be at your own home or that of a friend or relative, and the smaller project will be done right here. There's a list of project ideas in your syllabus that will start your brains turning. Please email me your project proposals by next Friday for approval."

Violet raised her hand. "How are we going to know what tools we should be using or materials we should be buying for our projects?"

"Why don't we all go shopping together at the local hardware store?" Sonya suggested amidst the concerned murmurs of the women.

Trent snapped his fingers. "Brilliant idea. Why didn't I think of it myself?"

"Probably because most men hate to shop," Sonya mused, and everyone burst out laughing.

Trent cast her an amused grin, and she was relieved that he'd taken her harmless comment in stride. He seemed to be the type of guy who would be patient with her and with everyone. He was easy on the eyes, too, and would provide some much-needed distraction on a weekly basis. Taking the class had been the right decision, and for the first time in a long while, she relaxed.

Trent locked the door to the workshop. Since his was the last class of the day, he'd been given a key. He wasn't sure he'd call his first day of teaching a class a success, but at least he'd gotten through it.

He knew the name of the mysterious woman he'd collided with in the coffee shop. He also knew that was where the association would stay. There were a lot of pretty women in the class, which made it even stranger that Steve had shoved his duties on to him.

"On second thought," Trent muttered under his breath, "it's better this way." While Trent preferred to date women who did not live in Bay Point, his brother held the opposite point of view. Steve's scandalous relationships had gotten the Waterson family named dragged through the rumor mills more times than Trent cared to count.

He slung his backpack over his shoulder. After class, he'd been surrounded by his students, all jostling for attention, that he'd lost sight of Sonya. He wasn't sure he could wait a week to see her again.

He'd instructed everyone to email him their contact info so he could send out a mass text message and email if he had to cancel class. He'd have

Sonya's info soon enough. What he didn't know was if she was single.

The class lasted twelve weeks. That was plenty of time to get to know her in a setting that took the pressure off both of them. He felt certain there had to be a rule at the college that he couldn't date the students he was teaching. The possibility almost made him want to quit, but then there would be practically no chance that he would see her again.

"Unless I decided to take up ballet," he said to himself.

He'd read about athletes who did ballet as part of their exercise regimen, claiming the results were both physically challenging and therapeutic.

That kind of dancing just wasn't for him. He was too wired most of the time and preferred to unwind with a cold bottle of beer and a fine woman at his side. The beer was easy to get. The woman? Not so much. Although, he sensed many of the women in his class would have gladly volunteered.

Lifting weights at the gym kept him healthy. Staying away from his brother kept him sane. And dreaming about falling in love with the perfect woman kept him hopeful.

He thought about Sonya, how her eyes had lit up with curiosity when he'd looked at her. He saw a flicker of hope there, too; he didn't know what it meant, but he aimed to find out. Maybe his search was finally over. Maybe hers was just beginning.

All he wanted at that moment was to discover the answers together.

When he reached the garage, he smiled. The sight of his motorcycle spelled freedom in his mind and in his heart. Riding was the ultimate escape. He became one with his bike, revving it up, driving it ever forward, bracing his body against the forces of the elements. He looked forward to every moment he spent on his classic motorcycle, and it was worth every penny he'd spent on it.

He took his black leather jacket out of his backpack and slipped it on. After making sure his backpack was secured, he put the key into the ignition, turned it and revved the engine. The low and raucous sound reverberated off the cement walls and echoed back into his ears. Although there weren't too many vehicles in that section of the garage, he heard the beeping of an alarm.

He revved the engine a few more times, slipped on his helmet, fastened it and slowly backed out of the parking spot.

He'd parked on the third level of the four-story garage and was rounding the curve toward the second level when his stomach rumbled. He planned to grab a bite to eat and then take the Pacific Coast Highway to his home just outside of town.

His heart flapped like a caged bird in his chest when he spotted Sonya waving her arms above her head. While she didn't appear to be hurt, she did need some kind of help and he was eager to assist.

He rode up alongside her and put his feet down on the pavement, stopping the cycle.

"What's the trouble?"

There was little chance of her recognizing him with the flap down on his helmet, and when he spoke his words were slightly muffled.

She cupped her hand behind her ear. "What? I can't hear you."

He unbuckled the strap of his helmet and lifted it off his head.

"And you thought you'd never see me again."

Her eyes widened. "Hiding again, Mr. Waterson?"

"What do you mean?"

She folded her arms across her chest. "You never told me you were a teacher when I spilled coffee all over you."

"How could I? I didn't know you were going to be my student."

He revved his engine by habit, and she clapped her hands over her ears.

"Don't you like motorcycles?"

She shook her head and frowned. "Not particularly."

Trent looked behind him and saw a car turning the corner and heading his way. He pedaled the cycle out of the way and turned off the engine.

"Why not?"

She dropped her hands to her sides.

"They're dangerous and loud, and the guys who ride them are usually trouble."

He laughed. "They are only dangerous in the wrong hands."

"I'm glad we agree on something."

"You think I'm trouble, huh?"

Sonya edged out a smile. "You could be."

"Thank you. I take that as a compliment. Now, what seems to be the trouble?"

She pointed to a little red convertible. "My car won't start."

He hopped off his bike and whistled. "She's a beauty, and I'm not just talking about the car.

"That's a pretty rare model, dating back to the late 1960s, correct? How do you happen to own one?"

"My father gave it to me for my sixteenth birthday."

"Very nice."

He heard the pride in her voice and it pleased him. It wasn't often that he met a woman who had an interest in cars, other than as a way of getting from point A to point B.

"It was a bribe to try and get me to major in business administration in college."

"From the look on your face, I'm gathering it didn't work."

"No, I majored in dance and enjoyed every minute of it."

"The color suits you."

"Thank you, I just wish it would start."

"Did you call for a tow?"

She shook her head. "No. My phone is dead and besides, this requires a flatbed truck."

"Hand over the keys and let me try."

She turned toward her tiny car and then back, sizing him up. "Are you sure you'll fit?"

A smile crossed his lips. "Worth a try, isn't it?"

She gave him a keychain that had a miniature cable car dangling from it. By the weight of it, he could tell it was pure silver.

"Okay. Give it a shot."

He opened the door and sat down, but his long legs wouldn't fit. "Snug."

"You might want to adjust the seat."

"Right."

He pushed the seat back as far as it would go. His knees were still cramped, but the fit of his six-foot-two frame was much better. He depressed the clutch with his right foot, stuck the key in the ignition and turned.

"Not even a click," Trent muttered.

"Told you so," she said, and couldn't help giggling. "Would you do me a favor and call for a flatbed tow?"

"I know just the guy for the job."

He tugged his phone out of his jacket pocket and put it to his ear.

"How soon can he be here?" she asked after he ended the call.

"Five or ten minutes. He's already in the area."

He got out of her vehicle and dropped the keys into her upturned palm.

"After he's done, I'll be happy to give you a ride home."

She gave him a wary look. "On that thing?"

Trent patted the seat. "Hey, you're talking about my best friend. Don't worry. We'll both treat you with the utmost care."

A grateful smile crossed her face, but her eyes were still distrustful. "Thanks, but I'm not sure I'll feel safe on a motorcycle. I've never ridden on one before."

Trent felt his heart pound against his chest, and he wondered why he felt a sudden need to change her mind. If it were anyone else, he wouldn't have cared. Why Sonya?

"I carry around a spare helmet, just for special occasions like these."

"Special?"

"Yes. It's not often I'm in the position to offer a trade."

"What do you mean?"

"Ride for ride. I give you a ride home on my sexy bike and you take me for a ride in your sexy convertible."

She paused and seemed to consider his offer. "Promise you won't go too fast?"

He held out his hand. "Deal. Let's shake on it."

Sonya took it, and he loosened up a little on his powerful grip so he wouldn't hurt her. He wished he didn't have to let go of her hand, but he did.

The tow truck arrived, and Trent helped the driver load up her car. When they were alone again, he opened up the case strapped to the back of his cycle that held two full-faced helmets. He picked up the spare and held it out to her.

"Go ahead, try it on. You're actually the first person to wear it."

"The fit is snug," she said. Her voice sounded muffled and a little bit fearful behind the visor. "Like it was made for me." Her hands trembled as she tried to fasten the strap underneath her chin.

"Allow me."

He fastened the strap and then flipped open the clear plastic visor.

"Your eyes are lovely, so to protect them from the wind and dust, be sure to put this back down again before we take off."

She nodded and gripped his wrist. "What do I do now?"

He glanced back at her and grinned. "Climb aboard, hold on and don't let go."

She hesitated for a few moments, and he could almost see the wheels of decision turning in her brain.

He wondered if she was a risk-taker, or was she one of those women who questioned everything?

When she settled in behind him and held on tight, he breathed an audible sigh of relief. A smile of triumph crossed his face, and he allowed himself to hope, after the ride was over, that he would see her again.

Chapter 3

Sonya straddled the seat and took her place behind Trent. Though her muscles were limber from years of dancing and yoga, the simple movement felt foreign to her. The rumble of the motorcycle's engine vibrated throughout her body. It seemed to hone in on her loins, adding to her excitement.

I must be nuts, she thought, but it was time to reclaim her life.

She'd defied her father's wishes and left Bay Point when she was seventeen years old. Their relationship, already on shaky ground, had deteriorated completely. Since then, she'd avoided taking risks in her personal and private life. Over time, she had suffered

a few injuries due to the strenuous training and performance schedule. The decision to teach had been
hard, but it was necessary if she wanted to continue
in her profession. She'd also found the courage to end
a relationship with a man that had run its course and
was going nowhere.

When she moved back to Bay Point, she'd vowed
to find a way to forget about her past and get back to
focusing on her new life. If part of the process was
a motorcycle ride from her instructor, then so be it.

"Get a little closer, will you? I don't want you to
fall off."

She touched her helmet and scooted forward,
keeping their bodies only a couple inches apart. She
placed one hand and then the other on each side of
Trent's waist. Her lips lifted into a tiny smile. Holding on to Trent from behind felt safer somehow. He
couldn't see the pleasure on her face, and she didn't
want him to know how much she enjoyed touching
him. Once again, she wished she could slip her hands
under his shirt so she could finally feel his skin.

"All set," she said loudly, so he could hear her
over the engine.

Without warning, the motorcycle lurched forward, crushing her breasts against his back. Her
arms looped around his waist and briefly settled on
the tops of his hips, before she jerked them away.

"Hold on," Trent commanded in a gruff tone without looking back. "I don't want any accidents."

"I will, and there won't be any, as long as you go slow," she retorted.

"I have to start moving in order to slow down, don't I?"

She couldn't respond. She was too busy trying to resist the urge to lay her cheek against the middle of his back, where the leather stretched over his shoulder blades.

He glanced over his right shoulder, a slight grin on his lips, as he revved the engine again. "Are you scared?"

The delicious thrum of the motor against her inner thighs and the challenge in his voice made her close the gap between their bodies.

"Not a bit," she assured him, even though her heart was in the pit of her stomach.

"Good, because I would never hurt you."

At his words, her heart melted. His body heat radiated through his clothes, and his masculinity draped around him, heavy and comfortable. She sensed she could snuggle up in his arms, fall asleep and not have to worry about a thing.

How she wished she could sweep everything that kept her up at night away from her mind, replace them all with a man that would sweep her right off her feet. She wasn't looking for it, but she never stopped hoping for a second chance at love.

She inched even closer, until her... She could feel his abdomen tense up.

Oh, my, she thought, with a lick of her lips.

His muscles were deeply ridged. It was as if she could climb a mountain and grab on to them so she wouldn't fall.

"That's better," he said in a gruff tone. "Hold on as tight as you'd like. I won't mind."

She nodded, inhaling the scent of his leather jacket. She had visions of him wearing it, and nothing else.

"Would you like to join me for a burger? It's way past my dinnertime and I'm starving."

She pursed her lips. "I thought you were going to take me home."

"I will, right after we eat."

She gave him a reluctant shrug, even as her curiosity to learn more about him was getting stronger.

"I don't have much choice, do I? You've got me captured."

He turned around. "I get the feeling that if you didn't want to be here, you wouldn't be.

"Then again, maybe it's just fate," she interjected.

He grinned and revved the engine. "You can tell me where you live when we get to the restaurant. I'm shy and I don't know how to make conversation."

She didn't ask him where they were going, allowing him to take the lead and surprise her. The college was located east of Bay Point in a residential neighborhood, and the dining options were limited to fast food and strip-mall takeout.

She figured the most likely destination was downtown Bay Point, which, much to her delight, had been revitalized in recent years with an influx of new restaurants and shops. Most of which she'd been too busy to try.

When they reached Magnolia Avenue, which led west to downtown Ocean Avenue, Bay Point's version of Main Street, Trent hooked a left and continued east. The road and the area was unfamiliar territory to Sonya, but she felt perfectly safe with Trent.

Tiny stars were just beginning to pop in the twilight sky as they rode silently through the moist autumn air. She wanted to open the flap of her helmet to smell the fresh air, but she didn't dare let go of Trent.

What does a man think about when he's totally alone? Wearing his helmet made her feel close to him, even though his thoughts and feelings were unknown to her. She was glad to have it.

About ten minutes later, they turned onto a gravel driveway. The roadside bar had no sign. Motorcycles and pickup trucks cluttered the parking lot. In the windows were colorful neon images of a martini glass, a bottle of champagne with the cork exploding and a frothy mug of beer.

In spite of the place's quirky appearance, Sonya's anticipation grew as Trent angled his cycle into a space. Before she knew what was happening, he was off the bike, and she took his hand as he assisted her.

She removed her helmet, handed it to him, and he put them both in the case and locked it.

She brushed her fingers through her flattened curls to bring them back to life.

The front door of the bar opened, and a man half walked, half stumbled out on the raucous notes of a classic rock tune from a jukebox.

He held the door open for the couple. "Enter, beautiful ones!"

Sonya blushed. Although she appreciated the compliment, the guy was obviously drunk.

"Thanks, man," Trent said, a smile on his face. "Do you need a ride home?"

"Nope. Rocky took my keys and called me a cab."

Trent patted the guy on the shoulder. "Good. Enjoy the rest of your evening."

They stepped over the threshold and heads turned.

"Hey, Rocky, got a table for two weary travelers?"

The bartender nodded and pointed to a dark corner. Many in the attractive, diverse crowd shouted hello and waved in their direction as they walked to the back of the restaurant.

Sonya nudged his elbow and he leaned in so close she could smell his aftershave. "Do you know everyone here?"

He put his arm around her as they shuffled

through a glut of people dancing. "No, but they know me, apparently."

Sonya wasn't sure if that was good or bad. Could it have to do with him being a so-called heartbreaker? She made a mental note to ask him later.

Trent pulled out one of the old bentwood chairs so that she could be seated first, impressing her with his old-school chivalry. The table was scarred with a variety of initials carved into the polished wood, and a couple of quotes that made her cheeks get hot.

"Are you sure we're going to get out of here alive?" she asked, only half joking.

"You are perfectly safe here with me. I got you here, didn't I?"

She arched a brow and folded her arms.

"I didn't have much choice, did I?"

He reached over and lifted her chin with the pad of his thumb.

"Yes, you did. And in my opinion, you chose wisely."

A waitress came by and dropped off a couple of menus and two waters, heavy on the ice.

Trent sat back in his seat as the woman stood there pen in hand. "Everything is good here, but I prefer the veggie burger and fries. Sound good?"

Sonya made a point to peruse the selections, even though his choices were not unlike something she'd choose for herself on a Friday night of fun when she didn't have a performance.

Before she could nod in agreement, Trent gave the waitress their orders and Sonya reluctantly gave up her menu.

When they were alone, Trent frowned, as if he'd just realized his mistake. "I'm sorry. I should have given you more time."

Sonya tapped one finger on her lips. "Let me guess. You're the kind of guy who acts first and begs forgiveness later."

"Bingo. Would you call that being arrogant or bold?"

"Will I get an F if I tell the truth?"

"No, but will it make you feel better if I told you this was the first time I've ever taught a class? I'm making this up as I go along. You won't tell, will you?"

She shook her head. "I guess we've both had a rough first day."

"I do want to thank you for suggesting the hardware store field trip. It really makes sense."

"You're welcome."

An attractive man in a green-and-white button-down shirt and blue jeans stopped by their table. Without asking, he dropped in the space next to Sonya and turned toward her.

"Excuse me, beautiful. I don't mean to intrude, but I've got an important question for your man."

Before speaking, he'd taken a second to wave his left hand, the one bearing his gold wedding band, in front of her face. In her opinion, he was either very devoted to his wife, or feeling guilty for cheating.

Her eyes caught Trent's and he gave a rueful shake of his head as he introduced them.

"Don't mind this clown, Sonya. Dario is an old buddy of mine that I allow to tread on my last nerve," Trent replied good-naturedly.

"When are you going to lower the prices on those homes in that new development of yours, Waterson, so that guys like me can afford them? I'm tired of my wife nagging me about it."

Dario's face registered no emotion, so Sonya couldn't tell if he was joking or serious.

Trent, on the other hand, seemed as uncomfortable as she had been when she'd first walked into the bar, like a stranger among friends.

"How much do the homes go for?" she asked.

"They start at a million and go up from there," Trent replied in a nonchalant tone.

"The base price of a Waterson home gets you four walls, a doorbell and that's about it," Dario replied.

Trent leaned back in his chair and shrugged his shoulders. "Welcome to the world of custom homes. Everything is an add-on."

Though Trent's words sounded good, his friend didn't appear convinced. In fact, he looked even angrier.

"You know that I don't set the prices. My brother

and my father do. I just build the houses to spec, on budget and on time."

"You're starting to sound like a salesperson. You know I'll never be able to buy one of your mega mansions, especially now."

Dario slammed one fist on the table and she jumped. A trickle of sweat ran down her spine as bad memories flooded her brain.

The tables were very close together, and Dario was blocking her only way out. The sense that she was trapped made her light-headed, and she knew she needed some fresh air right away.

She braced her right hand on the table and tried to stand up. "Excuse me, please."

Trent's palm closed over her hand, and she hitched in a breath. The warmth from his skin forced her to concentrate on his touch, instead of her panic. He mouthed the words, *It's okay*, motioning with his chin for her to sit back down, so she did.

Trent leaned in close and lowered his voice. "I'm sorry you were laid off from your job recently, but I'm a regular guy, just like you."

Dario folded his arms. "Who are you trying to convince? Me or you?"

Trent caught Sonya's eye before speaking.

"Don't go spreading this around town, but I believe we're looking into building homes with a lower price point. If that happens, you'll be the first to know. We'll be hiring local workers."

Trent's words diffused the tense situation, and the men shook hands. Dario tipped an imaginary hat toward Sonya and then left.

"Was that guy a friend or an enemy?"

Trent glanced over at the bar, where Dario saluted him with a full mug of beer, and back at her.

"I wish I knew."

"So guys have frenemies, too?" she chuckled, trying to lighten the mood.

"Yeah." He paused. "Can I ask you a question? You nearly hit the ceiling when he pounded on the table. I'm sorry that Dario's actions startled you."

He paused a beat, as if he expected her to explain.

"It just surprised me, that's all."

She didn't want Trent to think she was being overly sensitive, and it was too soon to talk about the reasons for her reactions.

She cupped her hand over her mouth and faked a yawn. "He definitely woke me up."

"I think there's more, but I'm going to let it go for now. Anyway, I'm sorry for the interruption. My brother makes me a lot of money, but he also causes me a lot of trouble. He's not the easiest man to like, or to defend."

"Aren't you a co-owner?"

"My father gave us equal control, but I'm more comfortable in a bulldozer than in the boardroom."

Sonya felt that invisible jolt inside when one connected with a kindred spirit.

She'd felt the same way when she was a ballerina. She didn't want to be bothered with the business side of things; she just wanted to dance.

"Are you really going to build more affordable housing?"

Trent folded his arms and rested them on the table.

"Let me put it to you this way. I think we should. But that doesn't mean we will. The only thing my father and brother care about is making money."

"And what about you?" she asked. "What do you care about?"

"Building custom homes that allow families to live their lives in a safe, secure community."

"Sounds like a viable mission statement."

"The difference is that I believe it and work it every day."

"Maybe I'll get to meet your brother one day."

"No, you won't. I want to keep you all to myself."

"Now who is being selfish?" she teased back.

"Do you have any brothers or sisters?" he asked.

She took a sip of beer. "I'm an only child."

"Are you a little emperor?" he teased, referring to the stereotype that only children were selfish because they had no siblings and never learned to share.

"No, but I'm the master of my own destiny."

"And what do you see in your future?"

She tapped her index finger on her lips. His question took her by surprise. Since high school, she'd had her life mapped out. Her plan had been to graduate from college, audition for a major dance organization, be accepted and spend the rest of her life onstage, retire early and then teach.

Somewhere along the way, as reoccurring injuries kept her sidelined, causing her to lose some key roles, she was forced to face a new reality. She knew that audiences were fickle, but didn't know that they could make or break a season. Many of her friends had gone on to other careers, because being a dancer simply wasn't sustainable. She never thought she'd be one of them, but here she was, back in Bay Point, living in her father's house.

"Let me see. I'd like to pass your class and get home in one piece, does that count?"

"I have it on good authority that both will come true."

"Are you a magic genie?"

He laughed. "No, just a man who has complete confidence."

After they finished their meal, Sonya excused herself to use the restroom while Trent paid the check. Outside, she gave him directions to her home. When he tried to help her with the helmet, she nudged his hand away.

"I think I can do this by myself now."

He shrugged his shoulders. "Suit yourself."

Sonya noted the hint of disappointment in his voice and figured that a man with his reputation wasn't used to having a woman say no. She wasn't helpless, just confused about all the feelings swirling inside of her.

When they arrived, she got off the motorcycle and handed him the helmet.

His eyes scanned over her house. "You've got a couple of shingles missing off your roof."

She followed his gaze, wondering how he'd spotted them, as she hadn't seen them before.

"I actually need to have the entire house inspected—inside and out."

"I can give you a few names to call, if you'd like."

"I'd appreciate that. Thanks for the ride, and for the dinner."

"It was my pleasure. When can I see you again?"

"Next week. Outside the hardware store, remember?"

He winked. "You're lucky I'm a very patient man."

As she watched him drive away into the night, she murmured, "You're going to be waiting a while."

As long as she kept this gorgeous man at arm's length, she could continue to figure out how she was going to live the rest of her life. Not as a dancer on a stage, but like a regular person.

No applause, no curtain calls and no encores.

Chapter 4

Trent groaned aloud as he pulled into the parking lot, wishing he could turn around and go somewhere he really wanted to be.

He drove past his reserved spot in the front of the two-story glass-walled building, a contemporary 1980s monstrosity that housed their multi-million dollar construction and real-estate business. He didn't like his family to see when he arrived, and he preferred to leave without notice.

He waved to a barista smoking a cigarette as he parked his pickup truck in the back of the building.

The family rented out the first floor to an independent coffee shop, and their offices were on the second floor.

They also owned and leased space in two equally large office buildings of the same contemporary style on either side.

He stayed away from the office as much as he could, but every week he had to attend a staff meeting.

Even though it was the middle of the morning, Trent grabbed an espresso before taking the elevator to the second floor. He'd rather be at the other end of a dental drill than at the weekly staff meeting or, even better, spending time with Sonya.

Trent chuckled to himself, and could hardly believe he was actually looking forward to teaching the home repair class, rather than dreading it.

He was still smiling as he pulled open the glass doors to the office. His brother, who was chatting with the receptionist, shot Trent a look of disdain.

"Couldn't you have changed your shoes before coming to the office?"

Trent glanced down at his muddy construction boots.

"I wanted to install a shower in the office, but you decided you needed your own personal bathroom with a full-length mirror and a jetted tub."

Steve spread his arms and grinned. "I'm here in the office so much it's practically my second home.

Too bad I can't say the same for you. Where have you been? I was trying to reach you all night."

"I was busy having a life. You could take notes from me."

Steve was older than Trent by two years, but he'd been blessed with a baby face complemented by dark caramel skin, which made him scorned by most men and desired by many women. It was his job to scout and acquire land for custom-home projects. On the side, he bought foreclosed and distressed properties for rehabbing and reselling, which fueled his habit for designer clothes, luxury cars and lavish vacations around the world.

"Ha ha. But seriously, I need you to hop on a plane to New Mexico."

Trent almost spit out his coffee. "What? Are you nuts?"

"Don't act like you didn't know that we're planning on expanding our portfolio to Albuquerque. I need you to go there and look at a plot of land."

"Sorry, no can do."

"Why not?"

"First of all, you know I can't stand flying. Second, I would never leave my projects halfway done, and last, I've got a class to teach."

"What class?"

Trent shot him a look, and Steve rolled his eyes.

"Oh, that one. Can't you skip it?"

"Like you did? Not a chance."

Steve patted him on the back. "I knew you could handle it, little bro."

They walked into the conference room where Lawrence and Agnes Waterson were already seated at opposite heads of the table.

His father was on a phone call, so Trent just shook his hand, and then he walked to the other end of the table to reach his mother.

He kissed her on the cheek. "Hello, Mom. Sorry I'm late."

Agnes Waterson, from whom he'd inherited his dark honey complexion, had just turned fifty and was an important balance of reason and influence in her testosterone-heavy clan. The petite self-ascribed people person enjoyed serving others in her role as director of marketing and human resources. She loved to spruce up the company's headquarter offices.

She returned a warm smile. "Good to see you. I heard you and your brother talking outside."

"Yes, he was asking me to fly, and he knows I hate to fly, and besides, I don't have the time."

"Come on, Mother," Steve cut in. "Even though I'm the first born, you always loved Trent more and thought he was a perfect little angel. He's got to have wings hiding underneath all that muscle somewhere."

"I love you both equally."

She got up to straighten one of the framed renderings of the developments that hung on the walls. "There's fresh coffee and muffins if you're hungry."

Trent stepped over to the antique mahogany side-board that Agnes had insisted be put into the conference room to lend the room an air of elegance.

Of course, Steve was already there, munching on the last banana muffin, which he knew was Trent's favorite. He settled for pumpkin, but only because he was really hungry.

Lawrence ended the conference call with an audible huff and a growl. He put his palms facedown on the table, as if he were about to stand up. Trent had long learned that was a habit, something his father did to steady himself after a difficult conversation. As president and CEO of Waterson Builders, he had plenty of those every day.

At six foot four, he towered over both of his sons and his wife, but never used his stature as a point of intimidation. It was when he stroked his neatly groomed salt-and-pepper beard that they all knew to brace themselves—not for yelling or screaming, but for tough questions. The company that he'd founded was his baby and he would do anything to protect its interests.

"What are you two boys squabbling about now?"

"Angel's wings, Dad," Steve said jokingly as he pulled out his chair and sat down.

"Here's something that's not very funny," his mother said. "Have you read the latest editorials in the *Bay Point Courier*? That's the first topic on our agenda today."

"No, and I don't want to hear it," Trent's father said, and Steve agreed with a nod.

Agnes threw up her hands in disgust. "You two are as stubborn as mules."

Trent sat down and began to thumb through the paper in front of him. "What's going on, Mom?"

"Backlash galore," she replied with a huge huff of a breath. "Everyone is complaining that our homes are too expensive, and out of reach for the average income-earning person."

"I don't know what the problem is," Steve muttered, placing his paper to the side. "Luxury homes are our business. We're not any different from any other company that services high-net-worth customers."

"I agree with Steve. We've been successful for over twenty years because our customers are overjoyed with their homes."

"There's even an editorial from Mayor Langston," Trent said, scanning the page. "He thinks it's our civic responsibility to build affordable housing. I'm actually surprised we haven't been called out before this."

"What is that supposed to mean?" his father demanded with a slam of his fist on the table.

Trent's tone was grim. "The luxury townhomes

and apartments downtown that were built during the period of revitalization can only be afforded by the wealthy. They're out of reach for many longtime residents of Bay Point."

"We're a private company, not a public institution. We are only accountable to ourselves and our customers," Steve piped in.

"Don't forget the hundreds of people we employ every day in Bay Point and other cities in the region," his mother added. "We play an important role in the local economy."

Trent took a few minutes to read the rest of the editorials, and when he was finished, he sat back in his chair.

"The voice of the people."

He thought back to his conversation with Dario the previous evening. He realized his attitude and response had been shameful. He could no longer stand by and do nothing.

"Give it a couple of weeks. With Trent in front of the classroom, and all the ladies ogling his good looks, I'm sure he will do his duty and speak positively about our company," Steve said smugly.

Trent croaked out a laugh. "If you're expecting me to be a walking billboard, Steve, you've got the wrong guy."

Trent was thankful for all the opportunities his family's company had afforded him and he loved his job, but there was always something inside of him that wished he could do more. Dario's comments and the editorials were the kick in the pants he needed.

"Besides, it explicitly states in the contract for adjunct instructors that we cannot promote a specific business," Trent said.

"Regardless, Waterson Builders only wants what is best for Bay Point."

"Yes, but we know the truth." Trent smirked.

Steve raised a brow. "And what truth is that?"

"We've only been focused on making money."

Steve and Lawrence glanced at each other and parroted, "And that's a bad thing?"

"I thought we were being charitable by offering free home improvement classes to help people to become more knowledgeable about home renovation. Isn't that enough?"

"It was a first step, Dad, and of course, it's not wrong to make money. However, it might do us some good to consider acquiring some land for the specific purpose of building affordable housing."

"I agree with Trent. We have to do more for the community. From a public relations perspective, it makes total sense."

"Spoken like a true marketer, Mom," Steve replied in a dry tone.

"If we do this, we do it right." He turned toward his brother. "We use the same high-quality materials that we do in all our other custom homes. No cutting corners."

"Fine." Steve sucked in a deep breath. "We'll have to get the land for cheap."

His father wore a grim look. "That won't be easy. I may not agree with all of Mayor Langston's policies, but his revitalization efforts have paid off. Bay Point has become one of the most popular places for relocation, and as a result, land prices have skyrocketed."

Steve turned to his mother. "Which is why we've been forced to expand outside of California. If Trent won't go to New Mexico, can we hire someone who will?"

Mother waved away his comment and said cheerily, "I'll go. I can videoconference everyone in via phone. We can all take a look at the land together—virtually."

She tapped her chin and looked around the room. He could almost see the wheels grinding away in her brain.

"I've been thinking about redecorating this place, anyway."

The three men groaned. If there was one thing they all could agree upon, it was that their mother would travel anywhere, anytime to go shopping.

"I guess it's all settled," Steve said. "I'll start putting out feelers today for available land in Bay Point."

Agnes waved a finger, and whenever she did, everyone listened a little harder. "No. I think we'd better keep this hush-hush, until we are ready to make a formal announcement."

"She's right, son. You better take care of this yourself," his father commanded. "Now, we all have a lot of work to do today. Let's move on to the rest of the agenda."

Steve, who normally worked through his posse of brokers, grumbled under his breath. He did not look happy at the prospect of doing the legwork on his own, and Trent wasn't sure if he even knew how.

At the end of the meeting, Trent stuck around for a few minutes to catch up with his mother.

"So, when are you going to bring a nice girl home for me to meet?"

Trent laughed at the question, which was a running joke in the family, although his brother didn't think it was so funny. Every time he brought a girl home to meet his parents, the woman took one glance at Trent and changed her mind.

Both men were handsome, but Trent believed he had something that his brother did not—integrity.

"Do you want to start another feud?"

"Of course not," she replied. "I just figured that as soon as one of you get married, you'll both stop squabbling."

Trent shrugged. "You're probably right, but when I tie the knot, I want it to be right. Steve falls in love with a woman as easily as he does his own reflection."

"Be nice," Agnes warned. "Your brother is just lonely, that's all. Even though he wouldn't dare admit it."

"Like he wouldn't dare admit he's the hottest guy in Bay Point, or so he claims?" Trent replied.

"He's just confident," his mother sniffed. "You both would have been married long ago, if you weren't workaholics."

"I'm in no rush. I want my marriage to be as successful as you and Dad's."

"We've had our rocky times like all marriages do," Agnes said. "Lawrence is my best friend. That's why I'm able to work with him, day in and day out, plus be his wife."

Trent nodded and kissed his mother on the cheek. Though he understood her wish for him to be in a relationship, at the moment there was something more important on his mind.

He tried to recall land in the area where, as he traveled to and from his job sites, he might have seen a for-sale sign. It was a short list. He jotted the addresses down and handed them to Steve. Though his brother thanked him, Trent would just have to wait and see if he used it or not.

He left the office, excited about the prospects of

working on what could be one of the most important community developments they'd ever done.

He pulled out his phone to check his email and see if Sonya had sent her contact information, as he'd instructed all of the students to do. Many of them had, but not her.

After a frustrated groan, Trent closed his eyes. A sad fact occurred to him. There was no woman he cared about deeply enough to share the good news in his life. That had never really bothered him until now.

Sonya was off-limits for a serious relationship, at least until the class had concluded. If her car hadn't broken down, he wouldn't have had the opportunity to spend an evening with her.

He turned on the ignition and thought about the missing shingles on her roof. He wasn't a licensed inspector, but he could have offered to take a look at the interior and exterior of her home himself.

He'd been waiting his entire life for the right woman to cross his path. Now, all he had to do was discover if that woman was Sonya.

Sonya plucked some stray sticks from the front yard, just for something to do, while Liza Marbet, a local architect, gathered her thoughts.

The two women had met in line at Ruby's Tasty Pastries, a popular bakery in Bay Point, and had struck up a conversation. They'd decided to have coffee together and became friends.

It saddened her that she'd been so busy trying to build her dance career that she'd lost touch with her childhood friends. Most of them had moved away. Although Liza was very busy, she'd agreed to take a look at the house and give her opinion.

The wind was calmer than her nerves as the afternoon sun filtered through the tall California sycamores dotting the front yard.

She didn't know why she was so anxious. Maybe it was because when she thought about all that had to be done, there was a tickle of regret that she'd even undertaken the responsibility at all. Her temples pulsed every time she thought about the eight-hundred acres of land behind the two-story farmhouse-style home.

She deposited the twigs into a larger pile under the tree, and then she walked up the stairs to the porch. After washing her hands, she returned outside.

Her mood turned ambivalent when she thought about the memories within those four walls, some good, some not so good. Over the years, she'd dealt with both in her own way. Now that she was no longer dancing professionally, Trent Waterson could be the perfect distraction.

"This house has good bones," Liza announced, joining her on the porch.

Sonya exhaled in relief and gestured to one of the wicker chairs. "You really think so?"

"Yes, but you should get a professional inspection of the interior and exterior."

She poured two glasses of iced tea and handed one to Liza. "I got some recommendations from someone in town."

Liza sat down and raised a brow. "Who from?"

Sonya hesitated for a moment. "Trent Waterson."

Liza waved a hand in front of her face. "Uh-oh, handsome and single."

"That's a bad thing?"

"Not at all. I actually know him well. He and his crew bulldozed an old motel to make way for my husband's cosmetic surgery clinic. He's very professional. How did you meet him?"

"He's teaching a class on home repair for women at the community college. I thought I would try to do some of the work around here myself."

"And start your dance studio at the same time?"

Sonya issued a wry grin. "Multitasking at its best."

Liza peered over both armchairs and under the seat cushion.

Sonya furrowed a brow. "What are you looking for?"

"A bundle of energy," Liza said in a serious tone.

"With everything on your plate, you're going to need it. Are you thinking of selling?"

"No. My aunt says we've had some interested buyers in the past. The value is in the land."

"It's a lot of work for one person."

"Not really." Sonya laughed, even though she knew deep down it was true.

She raised her glass of iced tea in the air. "All I need is a hammer, some nails—"

Liza cut in and raised her glass, too. "And a man like Trent to get the job done right."

"No!" Sonya said sharply. "I can do this on my own."

Her voice softened at Liza's frown. "At least, I want to try."

Liza nodded and finished the rest of her iced tea before responding. "I understand. When I moved to Bay Point, it was a chance for me to do things my way. And I didn't want anything or anybody to prevent me from doing what I'd come here to do."

Sonya tapped the top of her head with one finger. It was a habit she'd developed over the years to check that her ballerina bun was neat and secure, most often prior to performances. Now, when she did that, the internal voice that whispered, *You're not performing anymore, and that's okay*, got stronger and stronger.

No one was watching or clapping or standing outside the stage door waiting for her autograph. She was an audience of one, responsible only for herself. That fact both scared and motivated her.

"Have you been successful?" Sonya inquired.

"Yes," Liza said and started to giggle. "I'm laughing because, at the time, I didn't think I would have any clients, and look at me. I'm so busy I can barely catch my breath."

"But you did catch a husband," Sonya teased.

"Oh, no, he caught me. Our relationship started out all business, but I think we both knew, deep down, that something special was brewing between us."

"You're a lucky woman, and a soon-to-be mom!"

"Thank you. I didn't expect to fall in love with my client, but I did, and I'm gloriously happy." Liza patted her baby bump. "What about you and Trent?"

"I hardly know him." Sonya widened her eyes. "He's just a guy who happens to be teaching my class and who happens to be—"

"Available," Liza said. "At least that's what I've heard."

Sonya made a sound in the back of her throat. "I was going to say, very experienced."

"Oh, how would you know?" Liza asked, flashing a lighthearted smile.

"I don't, unfortunately, but I wish I did." Sonya covered her mouth. "Oh, my goodness, did I just say that?"

Liza grinned. "You bet you did, and I can't blame you. If I weren't married, I would go for him. He's gorgeous, and a really good guy, from what I've heard."

Sonya thought back to Violet's comment at the first class, but she wouldn't dare repeat it. She wasn't a gossiper, like many of the people in town.

"That's good to know," she murmured. "But I don't have time for a relationship right now."

"So where does that leave me?" Liza asked with her hands on her hips.

Sonya burst out laughing. "Oh, don't worry. I have time for friends, just none for men." She extended a small tray of lemon biscotti to Liza, who selected one.

"A man like Trent could change your mind."

"Perhaps, but I'm not in a rush."

"One piece of advice?" Liza asked.

Sonya bit into a biscotti and nodded. "I'll take it."

"If it feels right, don't question it and don't wait. True love works on its own timetable."

"How will I know?"

"Trust me, when you fall in love with the man you're supposed to be with, you won't even have to ask. You'll just know."

She thought about Dewayne, the man who she'd thought she loved and felt a rush of guilt. She'd lost count of how many times he proposed, and each time, she refused. She guessed she had a touch of heartbreaker in herself, so how could she possibly judge Trent?

Liza snagged another biscotti from the tray. "So do you miss life as a ballerina? It must have been so exciting."

"It was, at first, a dream come true, but the reality was that the only thing I had control over in my career were my own two feet.

"Ow!" She slipped off her tennis shoes. "It's not as glamorous as everyone thinks."

"Whoa," Liza exclaimed. "Your feet are…"

"Beat-up, I know," Sonya exclaimed, more from the sudden pain, than Liza's comment. "Battle scars."

She grabbed some massage oil from a small table on the porch. She kept the small bottles scattered around the house so that she could address the pain whenever and wherever it struck without warning.

"Sorry. Do you mind?" Sonya asked. She slathered some on her feet. "I usually walk around barefoot at home, because I never know when the pain is going to hit."

She crossed one leg over her knee, and then the other, rubbing her feet until the pain subsided. She refused to take medication, preferring the healing balm of touch.

"That must be awful."

"Yoga helps a great deal." She gritted her teeth and flexed her red-painted toes. "So do pedicures."

Liza tapped one finger to her lips. "Hmm, I wonder if Trent gives good massages."

"You're evil," Sonya joked. She wiped the oil from her hands with a clean tissue. "What am I supposed to do, just go up to the man and ask him to work his magic on my ten little piggies?"

"Ha! Just promise me that you won't put a damper on any of his attempts to woo you. I'll bet he'll surprise you."

Sonya got up and brushed the crumbs from her lap and invited Liza inside to talk about design treatments for the interior of her home.

For the first time today, she doubted her friend's words. Other than Dewayne, Trent Waterson was probably just like any other man she'd ever dated. Sweet and caring all the way until he got her into bed, and then unavailable and aloof when he got out of it.

Sonya was used to pain, both emotional and physical.

When she was a little girl and a beginner student at Miss Celia's House of Dance, she did her first pirouette in her pretty pink ballet shoes and her heart had been full of joy. Her mother had applauded with enthusiasm and proud tears in her eyes, but her father had not. He just looked angry.

One night, after a performance, she'd overheard an argument between her parents. While her mother insisted that Sonya was learning poise and grace, which would serve her well as she grew up, her dad felt like too much money was being wasted on lessons and costumes, with too little to show for it.

Though her heart was torn to pieces from the lack of acceptance from her father, she'd refused to cry or give up her love for dance.

Whenever she thought about giving up on anything, she channeled the same energy and will to succeed that she'd had as a child. Her plan now was to stay focused on fixing up her property and making her new business a success. There would be little time for a relationship, and, therefore, even less chance to be hurt.

Chapter 5

Sonya watched red and gold leaves chase each other down the middle of Ocean Avenue as she waited in front of Sal's Hardware. She had hoped that the store would open early so that she could navigate the aisles before Trent and the rest of the class arrived. But although the lights were on, the door was still locked.

A sudden breeze swirled granules of sand from the sidewalk around her feet as she peered in the shop window. There were a variety of small tools hung up on a beige pegboard, an old-fashioned rusty push mower, as well as a small sign advertising 20 percent off paint and painting supplies.

She bit her lip with worry, wondering what she

would do when the store opened, besides walk up and down the aisles in an utter fog. The decision on what project she should tackle first still befuddled her, so she hadn't emailed her choice to Trent. Nor had she provided her contact information.

She was officially late on two assignments, something that had never happened to her before. She was the kind of student that always turned everything in either early or on time. Her stomach flipped in a mix of annoyance and anticipation. She'd been an A student all through high school and college, and even though this was a pass/fail class, she wanted to do well.

Old-fashioned copper streetlamps with the blue-green patina of age lined both sides of the two-lane road. She stepped out from under the store's red awning and leaned against one, turning her face eastward.

The sun's warmth always made it seem like nothing could go wrong with her day. The beaches of Bay Point were close by, and every time she inhaled the salty air, it renewed her spirit more than the most strenuous yoga positions.

"Falling asleep on me already?"

Her eyes snapped open at the low baritone voice floating toward her.

Trent held up a plain white, green-sleeved paper cup she recognized from Ruby's Tasty Pastries.

"This should help keep you awake. Regular roast,

two creams, no sugar, but only if you promise not to spill it on me this time?"

He bowed, and she found the gesture charming, despite his reference to the way they'd first met.

"And ruin your pristine white T-shirt? Not a chance."

She wouldn't want anything to get in the way of the fabric that stretched perfectly across his well-formed pectorals, moving with him as he lifted his arm to take a sip of his coffee.

"Do you like it?" he asked, his lips turned up into a smile. "I wore it just for you."

She forced herself to look away from his upper body and into his eyes. "Very sweet of you," she beamed as she took the cup from him, deliberately trying to hide her pleasure, but knowing she was probably not doing a very good job of it.

"How did you know what I liked?"

"Which one, the shirt or the coffee?"

Sonya rolled her eyes. "The java, of course."

"I asked the owner herself."

Ruby was famous around town for her ability to remember the likes and dislikes of her regular customers. It was one of the reasons why her shop was so popular, besides the delicious baked goods.

"Ah! How could I have forgotten?" Sonya flipped open the tab on the cover and took a careful sip. It was hot and tasted delicious, but it needed pastries to make it perfect. "No buttery croissants, no apple-crumb danish?"

"Demanding, aren't we?" He grinned and pointed to a warning sign on the front of the store. "No food, no pets."

"No shirt, no service," she finished aloud. "Too bad." She frowned.

"Which part of that disappoints you the most?"

"Since I don't have a pet, no food," she responded with an innocent smile.

"Is there a reason why you're wearing such a pretty dress to the hardware story today? Are you going to a party afterward, or on a date?"

"Neither." She leveled her gaze at him and kept her tone serious. "I wear dresses as often as I can. I love the freedom of movement they give me."

She took a step forward and almost twirled around to show him what she meant, but decided it was wiser to step back under the protection of the awning.

"You look beautiful in it."

She hitched in a breath at his compliment. "Are you flirting with me?"

"Yes, is there a reason why I shouldn't?"

She gave him a sweet smile. "Aren't you afraid of being seen as playing favorites? Bringing me a coffee, choosing your clothes just to impress me."

He held up his hands. "Is that a crime? There's nobody here but you and me. Besides, class doesn't start for another ten minutes. Why are you here so early? Could it be that you missed me?"

"Is there something wrong with being punctual?"

"Not at all, I was just hoping it was because you missed me."

"I don't like school that much," she teased. "But I always loved field trips when I was a kid. I guess that's one reason why I suggested this visit to the hardware store in class. I'm almost ashamed to admit I've never been in one. I lived in a luxury apartment in San Francisco, so any repairs were taken care of by the management company."

Whenever something was broken, her father had always hired a repairman, but only after he'd attempted to fix it himself. She chuckled inwardly to herself, realizing that was one thing they had in common. There wasn't much else.

"I've been coming to Sal's since I was a little boy. He used to sell these toy tool belts, and I would ride my bike downtown after school and stare at them in the window. The best Christmas I ever had was when I found one under the tree."

Sonya wondered what Trent was like as a little boy. "Is that what got you interested in building things?"

"No, it was just something I needed to do. As a kid, I was constantly stacking things on top of one another, like blocks or those little wooden logs. I have a degree in construction engineering, but I prefer to be hands-on, building the homes of my customer's dreams. I guess I just wanted to make a mark in this world."

"That's wonderful. It sounds like you're happy with your choice of career."

He nodded. "It's hard work, but I am. Maybe someday I'll show you a few of my projects and take you for another motorcycle ride. What do you say?"

Her heart beat just a little faster. Trent had just asked her out on a date, and even though she wanted to accept, she wasn't sure that she should.

"Maybe." She smiled. "But don't you think I should do my homework first?"

Trent wrinkled his brow in confusion, and she giggled.

"I didn't turn in my project idea, because there's so much to do in my house that I don't know what to start."

His face relaxed into a grin, and she knew he understood. "I can help you prioritize. Do you have the list with you?"

"No, that's the other thing. I left it at home."

"Even better, I'll stop by later and we'll look at it together. Okay?"

She nodded and the door opened. Sal DeNardo stepped out with a big smile and his arms open wide. He was the son of Italian immigrants who'd left the east coast over fifty years ago and made their way across the country to settle in Bay Point.

"Ah! It's my favorite customer in all of Bay Point."

He pointed his finger at Trent's chest. "Don't tell Steve."

Trent shook his hand. "Are you telling me that my brother has actually stepped over the threshold of this fine establishment?"

"No, of course not." Sal laughed and nudged Trent with an elbow. "But I hear the talk in town. There's no love lost between the two of you. Women aren't the only ones who gossip, eh?"

Sonya arched a brow. This was the second time she'd heard a reference to Trent's brother. She wondered what had caused the alleged rift between the two men.

Sal turned to Sonya. "And who is this pretty lady? Your girlfriend?"

Their eyes met, and she swore she saw a flame of heat in his gaze as he made the introductions.

"No, Sonya is one of my best students. Is everything ready to go for today's class?"

"Yes, right this way."

She heard the sound of female laughter. Sonya saw Violet and some of the other students heading their way, and she waved at the group.

Sal ushered them into the store and as he headed down one aisle, Trent hung back a bit and caught Sonya's elbow.

"I have a list of items that everyone should have

in their toolbox. I'll stop by your house later this afternoon to drop it off, okay?"

She nodded, and just as Violet opened the door, he let go. Sonya didn't think she saw, but his touch had been totally innocent, despite the pulsating heat it left behind.

Sonya pushed aside any worry about idle gossip and her project, and decided to focus on the excitement of the hours ahead.

Trent yawned as he traveled down Jacima Way, a winding, somewhat hilly road that led to Sonya's home.

A couple of times last night, he'd opened his laptop intent on doing some research about Sonya, but decided it would be better to learn more about her through good old-fashioned conversation.

She seemed guarded at times, which was understandable given her father's reputation in town. He'd just have to proceed slowly, allowing her to reveal as much, or as little, as she felt comfortable doing.

As he motored up Sonya's driveway and got his first look at her place in the daylight, it was clear that her dad had put very little, if any, effort into the upkeep of the home.

In addition to the missing shingles, the yellow clapboard appeared to be rotted away in some places, the porch sagged and the mortar between the bricks on the lower half of the home was crumbling. And that was just what he saw with his naked eye.

Five minutes, Trent told himself as he shut off the ignition. *That's how long I'll stay.* Otherwise, he might just grab his tools out of his truck and start fixing stuff.

Sonya appeared in the doorway before he put a foot to a step. She checked her watch. "You're early."

He bounded up the stairs with a grin and tipped an imaginary hat. "Just following your lead, ma'am."

The faded blue overalls rolled up at the ankles would have looked childish on most women, but on Sonya's lithe body, the effect was mesmerizing because of its nonelegance. She wore a red scoop-necked T-shirt and ballet flats that did not do a great job of hiding the faded purplish-bruises on the tops of her feet.

Trent whistled. "I'd expected a pink tutu, some taffeta and a little lace, but I think I like this better."

She looked down and laughed. "This old thing? It's my cleaning outfit."

She held open the screen door, which had been patched over in places. "Come on in, if you dare."

He let the door slam behind him, and found he was in the living room that smelled like fresh-cut lemons.

"Is there something I should be afraid of?"

"Take a look around and see for yourself."

There was a sofa, two easy chairs and a couple of

side tables, all mid-century vintage. He would never admit it to Sonya, but he was looking for signs that a man lived here with her.

"This is a big house for just one person."

"My aunt Nelda lived here for a while after my father passed away. She moved into an apartment recently but still has some things here."

"No boyfriends?"

"Who—me or my aunt?"

"Who do you think, silly?"

"My ex and I broke up a long time ago when I was still living in San Francisco. Satisfied?"

"I didn't mean to pry, Sonya. I just don't want to tread on somebody else's ground."

She anchored her hands on her slim hips. "You're here to give me advice, aren't you? Or are you here for something more?"

He waved his hands at his waist. "No, no. Nothing to see here, folks. This is just a friendly visit with the sole purpose to assist a fellow Bay Pointer in need."

Their eyes met and they smiled at each other, filling Trent with a sense of joy and relief. They both knew deep down that his visit today could be the start of something very special.

The focal point of the living room was a stone fireplace, swept clean of charred embers, with a low wooden bookcase flanked on each side.

"Does it work?"

She clasped her hands behind her back. "Yes, I

had it inspected. I haven't even used it yet, but I'm looking forward to it."

On the top of each bookcase, there was a smattering of family photos.

"Ours are like that, too." At her questioning look, he continued, "I'm talking about mismatched frames of various shapes and sizes."

"Have you ever seen those catalogs where you can buy a three-pack of frames in all the same shape?"

He took the liberty of picking up one heart-shaped frame, which contained a small image of a baby being cradled by her two parents. He assumed it was a picture of Sonya, and he handled it just as carefully.

"I always wondered why some people feel that the objects holding their memories have to be perfect. Families certainly aren't, right?"

"Mine wasn't," she replied bluntly. "Can you put that back, please?"

He set the frame back in its place, next to one that he assumed was her aunt. He took one last look at the baby photo, wanting to sear it into his mind, wanting her to explain more about her life growing up in this house.

He loved his parents deeply, but rarely did they see eye to eye. A lot of the times, he felt that if they didn't have the business, they would have split apart a long time ago. Not his mother and father, as they were devoted to each other, but he and his brother.

He hoped that in Sonya's case, the family dynamics weren't too painful for her, but he had a feeling that they were. And he wished that he could shake the feeling that he was starting down a road with Sonya that he might never want to end.

She stuck her hands in her front pockets and seemed nervous. Her voice was soft again. "I—I had to move those there from the mantel because it is loose. I think it needs to be fixed."

"Let's see what the trouble might be."

He jiggled the mantel with the edge of his hand, and the stone shifted only slightly. He looked underneath and spotted the problem right away, motioning Sonya for a closer look. Her perfume smelled like some exotic flower he would never remember the name of, but always made him want to hit a tropical beach and never go home.

"Look here. The screws in the metal brackets that hold up the mantel are rusted exactly where they are connected to the fireplace." He touched them and showed her some of the reddish dust that had collected. "That was the right thing to do. You can add this to the fix list."

"I have a handyman on speed dial. Unless of course, you only want me."

"Let me ask you something. Do you make house calls to all your students' houses to give them advice on their projects?"

"No, but..."

"I'm not looking for special treatment."

"If you haven't gotten the memo yet, I like you."

The smile she gave him lit up the insides of his soul. It was as if she'd never heard those three words before. Or maybe it was the first time she'd actually believed them.

Besides a large living room, there was a dining room and a kitchen with a cozy eat-in nook.

She handed him a list. "As you can see, there's a lot to be done."

The place was clean, comfortable and livable. So he wasn't sure why he hesitated before speaking. He could see why she was having trouble choosing what project to start.

"I thought about what you said in terms of keeping the project as easy as possible, and make it something that could be completed in a weekend."

"Yes, you are more likely to finish it."

"I've decided to paint the cupboards instead of replacing them."

"That's a great idea. What color?"

"I was thinking an antique white."

"I have some old cupboard doors that have glass in front that I salvaged if you're interested. It would give you a more open feel. I could repaint them and show you how to install them. Some vintage hardware would be the finishing touch."

"Wait a minute. It sounds like you want to do my homework. Isn't that called cheating?"

"Not when you're using it as an excuse to be close to someone."

"Are you always such a flirt?"

"Only when I believe my efforts will be fully appreciated by the other party." He bowed. "And only when I truly mean the words I say, which in this case, I do."

"Liza Marbet came to view the house several days ago and gave it the thumbs-up for having good bones."

He raised a brow and set the list back down on the table. "That's high praise. I'm working on a couple of jobs with her clients. She does the design and I build the house!"

He set the piece of paper back on the kitchen counter.

"I hate to add to the list, but I recommend energy-efficient windows, refinishing the floors, replacing the wallpaper with new paint, as the priority for repair and in that order."

"Those are all expensive projects. Can you suggest something more affordable that I can do?"

He thought a moment, and then snapped his fingers.

"The fireplace would be a good one. You could replace the stone mantel with one made of wood polished to a high shine."

"Do you really think I can do it?"

"Yes. I have a feeling you can fix a lot of things."

Like the loneliness in my heart. The admission in his mind, the utter truth that he needed someone, needed Sonya, nearly took his breath away. He was a master craftsman, an expert at building luxury homes, but he'd left building his own love story to fate.

Now was the time to explore the possibilities with Sonya. She was beautiful and sensitive, but most important, she was available.

The bay window in the kitchen provided a glimpse of the backyard and the rolling hills beyond.

"Would you like to go outside?" she asked.

They stepped out onto a small brick patio. "I can envision a deck back here with an extra-large grill."

"Another expense?" she moaned as they walked several feet away from the house.

"Hey, don't worry. I'll make the burgers. I am a good cook, as long as I'm not distracted."

And he knew he would be if he got into a relationship with Sonya. He wanted to tell her so, but instead, he shaded his eyes.

"It's gorgeous out here. I can see the white caps of the waves. How far are you from the Pacific?"

"Three miles. We still get the cool ocean breezes. This homestead has been in my father's family for over one hundred years."

"Did you ever keep horses or raise cattle? This land would be perfect. There's plenty of grass for grazing."

She laughed. "Me, personally? No, and no one in my family. I've never seen any reference to horse or cattle farming here. This land is beautiful, pristine and perfect."

So are you, Sonya.

His words were silent, but the meaning of them nearly rocked him off his feet.

He wanted to turn around and take her into his arms, but he held back. He needed to proceed with caution. Sonya's spirit and body were strong, but there was something else about her that was fragile.

He stood there awhile, inhaling the fresh air, surveying the rolling lush hills of Sonya's land, and his mind turned to business. It was untouched territory and, with its close proximity to downtown Bay Point and the ocean, could be an ideal consideration for residential development. It could be ideal for his company's first foray into affordable housing.

Would Sonya consider selling everything to Waterson Builders? Bringing this lead to his mother and father would prove that he could be effective on the sales side of the business.

The squeak of a hinge that needed oiling brought him back to attention. Sonya had snuck off to sit in a two-person swing, and he recognized it as one that could be found at any big-box home improvement store.

She had one leg tucked under her body and used

the other to push the swing. As soon as he sat down, she moved into a cross-legged position and faced him.

Her arms were lean and muscular, the kind that were only achieved due to a devotion to stretching and careful exercise.

"So do you think I'm crazy to have taken all this on?" she asked, spreading her arms wide.

"I admire you. Something must have brought you back. Most people come back home because they're either running away or running toward something. Which is it for you?"

Her arms fell to her sides. "This swing wasn't here when I left ten years ago."

"It's a more recent model. Maybe two or three years old."

"I often wonder why he bought it. He wasn't the type of man to stop and smell the roses. He kept very busy. If he wasn't working, he was…"

Her voice trailed off, but Trent had a feeling she was going to say that her father was gambling.

"Go on," he urged gently.

"I wonder if he sat here, gazed at the hills and thought about his life."

"Maybe he was trying to soak it all in. This view could give a person strength and courage. It's also very humbling."

"And maybe it was too late," she snapped.

A moment later, she covered her face with her

hands and began to sob. He wanted to take her in his arms, but he also didn't want her to lash out at him.

"If I said something wrong, I'm very sorry."

Tears flowed down her cheeks. "No, it's not you. I'm just trying to deal with the memories of my father."

He moved over and draped an arm over her shoulder, and she laid her head against his chest.

"Did you see that old tire out front? The one hanging from the sycamore tree? I can't bear to cut it down or get rid of it because that would be admitting defeat. That my father really didn't love me."

He realized he was on dangerous emotional ground.

"I didn't know your father. When he was alive and had the jewelry store, I never had an occasion to buy jewelry so our paths never crossed. I would never make assumptions about your relationship with him. I do know that no one deserves to feel unloved. I'm very sorry you're in such pain right now."

His eyes were luminous with desire. "I barely know you, but I want that to change. Do you?"

She gazed up at him under hooded eyes, and whispered, "Yes, I would like that very much."

He barely let her get the words out before he began to pepper her face with light kisses. She leaned into him as he nuzzled the base of her neck all the way up until his lips devoured her mouth.

Their tongues slid against one another as their

kiss deepened, and her low moan vibrated against his teeth.

The strap of her overalls fell down, and he broke away to lick the flesh of her exposed shoulder. Sonya leaned her head back and she shivered a bit in his arms as a gentle breeze stirred between them.

As she moved into a more comfortable position, the swing squeaked. The sound reminded him of bedsprings, and he wished he could set her on top of him and make love to her right there. The problem was, they were outside in broad daylight, and even though the property seemed secluded, he wasn't completely sure that it was.

Instead, he took her lips in his and unhooked the strap of her overalls with one hand. She began to breath a little more heavily, so he figured it was okay to proceed.

Cupping her breast in one hand, he discovered with delight and relief that she wore no bra. Furthermore, her nipples were hard as nail heads. His mouth began to water and he felt his penis spring to life. He wanted to touch her breasts, he wanted Sonya to feel how much he wanted her, but he paused, knowing if he proceeded, there was no turning back.

Sonya wasn't the type of woman who would be satisfied with a one-night stand. He felt that she would want to go slow, move cautiously, before giving herself to him. If he couldn't handle that, he should stop now.

But he didn't let go of her breast. He couldn't, because she'd placed her hand over his. With her permission, he began to stroke her nipple with the pad of his thumb, and she began to move her hips in tandem with his circular motion.

After a while, she put one hand behind his neck and guided his head slowly down to her chest, as she lifted her shirt with the other. He enclosed her breast in his hand and sucked greedily on her blue-black nipple, flicking it back and forth with his tongue.

"Baby, you taste delicious, and I'm just getting started."

"Go on," she panted, running her fingers through his hair. "Please, Trent, don't stop."

The swing squeaked every so often with his movements, heightening his excitement. He kept his pace steady as he sucked, taking his time, even though he wanted to devour her. He could tell that by the way she was squeezing her thighs together that she liked what he was doing, that she wanted more.

He gave her nipple a final tug before coming up for air. Sonya's eyes were closed, but she opened them as he pulled her back into her arms.

"So what do you think? Maybe there is still some room in your heart for a simple guy like me?"

Not to mention your bed. Although he had no problem waiting as long as it took to get there.

"There's no one special in my life right now. Maybe that will change. It's too soon to tell."

He held up his hand as if he were about to take an oath. "No problem. Like I said, I'm a patient man."

"I promise I won't make you wait too long," she teased in a sultry tone. "Now can we get back to that kiss?"

As he lowered his lips to hers, he realized he wasn't going to breathe a word about Sonya's property to anyone, least of all his brother.

Trent wasn't a superstitious man by any means, but he had a feeling that this woman could mean a lifetime of pleasure and happiness. He wasn't about to screw things up just as they were beginning.

Chapter 6

Sonya pulled into the garage and stole a last look in the rearview mirror. She'd invited Trent over to take a look at the second floor and the attic. It was an extremely bold request, but her excuse, which was pretty lame, was that they hadn't gotten around to it the other day.

Too busy making out.

It was funny how one little kiss, or a thousand of them, from a gorgeous man could change her whole outlook on life.

She giggled as she fluffed her hair, which had been freshly washed, trimmed and curled to perfection.

She'd spent most of her life concentrating on her appearance for the purposes of performance. After years of wearing her hair in a tight ballerina bun, it felt freeing to allow it to tumble forward around her face.

She did now, mussing it up a bit, and checked the mirror again. She liked it better that way. Life wasn't perfect—why should her hair be?

"I can just be myself," she declared to her reflection. "Messy hair and messed up feet and all!"

Saying the words was easy, but she knew she was going through a period of adjustment, with only herself to rely upon to make it to the other side.

Now that was a fact. She wasn't going to leave her future, good or bad, up to a man to decide. Her mother had fallen into the trap and suffered greatly for it. She'd given up everything for a man who hadn't appreciated her as much as she deserved.

She'd died when Sonya was just nine years old. She'd never seen her daughter achieve her dreams, just as she'd never achieved her own.

Sonya grabbed her leather tote bag out of the trunk and noticed the real-estate magazine inside. She'd read it in the salon, and the owner had allowed her to take it home.

The eye-catching pictures and inspiring descriptions had captivated her. Near the beginning of the publication, there was a six-page advertisement for

Waterson Builders, which had developments located in Bay Point and other nearby towns.

According to an accompanying advertorial, Waterson homes were some of the most expensive and highly sought homes in the region. The company was rapidly expanding by acquiring more land in the area and other states.

She pressed in her security code to close the garage door. As she made her way to the back door of the house, she saw her aunt sitting in one of the wicker chairs on the patio, reading the paper.

"Hi. How long have you been waiting?"

"Only about fifteen minutes," she sighed. "It's times like these when I wish I hadn't given you back my keys."

"You could have kept on, Aunt Nelda."

"No, that's all right."

"Have you had the locks changed?"

"Not yet. It's on my list."

"That's the first thing you should do when you move into a new home."

"It's not new, and besides, I've had the same keys for years."

"Then why didn't you use them? Why didn't you come home more often?"

"We've been through this a million times, Auntie. When I decided to leave Bay Point and follow my dreams instead of Dad's, that was it. I wasn't welcome here, remember?"

"My brother was so stubborn. Why did you even listen to him?"

"Because he was my father, and that's what I was taught to do."

"Sometimes, you can't follow the rules," Aunt Nelda said.

Sonya was surprised to hear those words. Other than her love for the blues, her aunt seemed to be the most strait-laced person she'd ever known.

She held open the screen door. "Won't you come in and have some lunch? I made a turkey yesterday and I have tons left over."

Sonya had a love-hate relationship with Nelda Young, her father's only sister. In her early sixties, she was a kind woman for the most part, but to Sonya, she was overbearing. Other than stiff joints and occasional back pain when she'd been on her feet too long, she was in good health.

"Are you here to pick up your last box? I brought it downstairs for you, and I can put it in your car."

"No, those are just odds and ends that I can get anytime."

Sonya hid a smile. This was the third time Aunt Nelda had said she was coming over to get the box. When she arrived, she always had an excuse on why she couldn't take it.

Sonya figured the real reason was because leaving it gave her an excuse to drop in anytime unannounced. She was Nelda's only niece and only living family member as far as she knew.

"The real reason I stopped by is that I have something important to discuss with you.

"As you know, when your father became older, he gave me power of attorney over all his affairs. And it was a good thing he did because quite frankly, you were too busy with your career to be bothered, and he knew that."

"Yes, and I agree, that was the right decision, at the time."

She'd hidden how hurt she had been that he hadn't considered his own daughter for the responsibility. He'd completely left her out of everything.

"And it worked for a while. He got stronger, but the pressure of everything he'd done right and, in his mind, wrong in his life weighed too heavily on his shoulders."

"What do you mean by wrong?" she asked.

"In his last days, he told me he was sorry he'd treated you the way he had in the months before you left for college. But more than that, he was sorry for all the time he'd missed with you growing up, because he was so busy working and—"

"Throwing all he worked for away by betting on sports?"

Aunt Nelda nodded sadly. "He died a peaceful death, but it was one full of regrets."

Sonya had her own barrelful of regrets that she

was trying to deal with on a daily basis. She should have been stronger and insisted on a relationship with her father.

When she'd walked out the door ten years ago, he had been angry, but he'd been alive and well. Ten years later, he was dead, and there was nothing she could say or do to let him know that, despite everything that had happened between them, she loved him.

"I appreciate you telling me, Auntie. But what was it that you needed to tell me today?"

"We agreed that I would retain ownership of the house for six months after I moved into my apartment. Legalities aside, I want you think of this place as your own home, at least for now."

"What do you mean, for now?"

"I never told you this, because I didn't want to upset you, but I used most of my savings to try and pay off your father's gambling debts, and we still lost the jewelry store. I'm afraid we're about to lose this place, too."

Sonya felt her face go slack with shock. "Lose our home. Are you sure?"

"Yes, your father took out second and third mortgages, both of which have been in default for months. Both banks have called the loans, which means…"

"They can foreclose."

"Exactly. There's no way I can pay them off."

"No, I don't expect you to. And if I'd known you

were trying to save Daddy's store, I don't know if I would have let you."

"Don't worry. I didn't give it all away. I was able to purchase my apartment, and my investments are sound."

"What about you? You're not really working right now."

"I put nearly all of my savings into the studio. I wish I would have known about the state of this place."

"You had to have known you couldn't dance forever. The studio is important. It's your nest egg for the future."

"Yes, but what good is it if I don't have a nest to reside in?"

"What can we do?"

"I don't want the bank to foreclose on the house, but our only choice to avoid it is to pay off the loan immediately."

Sonya felt torn. If this had happened ten years ago, she wouldn't have fought it. But now, even though the house required a lot of repair, she was looking forward to the possibilities of doing something with it, of making the house her own.

Being with Trent the other day had made the emotional pall that she always felt just being in the house nearly go away.

"They can't do that right away, can they?"

"It depends on the bank. I've read some horror

stories on the internet. By law, they have to keep us updated on the proceedings. But an auction can happen quicker than you might think."

"I think you and I just have to face facts. This home doesn't belong to the Young family anymore. It belongs to the bank."

"It belongs to our family, even if it is just us two. And we can't stop fighting for it."

Her aunt parted the curtains at the bay window in the kitchen. "It's a shame that the only people who will ever enjoy this view is you. If we sold this home, and the land with it, the money would be more than enough to pay everything off, and I'd recoup my losses from the jewelry store."

"No, Aunt Nelda."

"Why not?" She pointed at the repair list on the refrigerator door. "How much money and how many years do you think it's going to take to do all that on a dance teacher's salary? Too long. Your mother knew that all too well."

"My mother didn't care about the money she made. All she wanted to do was dance. That's what made her happy. At least until Daddy convinced her that she was wrong."

"Regardless, what are you going to do with eight-hundred acres of land? Why, someone else might be interested in it and could do a lot more with it than you or I ever could."

She was already committed to Bay Point, because

of her business, but not necessarily committed to her family's homestead. Still, she couldn't let it go yet.

"We can't sell. Don't do anything yet, Aunt Nelda. Let me get some advice and talk to an attorney."

"I realize you grew up here, but I have power of attorney over your father's affairs and I'm too old to deal with this anymore. If you want the house, this is going to have to be your fight, not mine."

Trent pressed the button at Sonya's front door and huffed out a deep breath at the church-bell chime.

He tried to ignore a gnaw of disappointment that she wasn't there to greet him. He hoped nothing was wrong.

He shifted his feet from side to side while he waited. His mother had always claimed he was a fidgety child and that he could never sit still. As he got older, he realized she was right. He never wanted to stay in one place, or with one woman. The fact that he was here with a small rose plant cradled in his arms was a revelation.

Besides the fact that she was a sensual kisser, Sonya already meant a great deal to him, for reasons he was excited to discover.

The door opened a crack, and then wider; although there was a smile upon her face, her complexion was ashen. Something was wrong. She appeared downright ill.

"Hello, Trent. It's nice to see you again."

Her words seemed forced and stilted, the opposite of the teasing banter they'd shared just a few days earlier.

He held up the rose plant. "I bought you this. I thought we could admire its beauty and yours over takeout from Lucy's restaurant."

She took a step back, as if she were shocked by his gesture. "Do you have a sixth sense?"

"No, I don't think so. Why?"

She pointed at the bag of food that he brought over. "Because I said I was going to cook you a meal, and I didn't. I meant to, but I've been sitting in one spot since my aunt Nelda left, and that's it. That's all I've been doing."

She wrung her hands together as he led her over to the living room couch. He set the bag of food and the plant down on one of the end tables. Facing her, he saw that her eyes were red-rimmed from crying.

"What's wrong, Sonya? Please tell me so I can help you."

Her chin dropped to her chest. "Thanks, but I don't think anyone can help me at this point." She lifted her head. "And you know what's the worst part? I told my aunt that I would take care of things, and I don't have the slightest clue how I'm going to do it."

Trent saw her hands were trembling, and he folded them into his. "Why don't you start at the beginning?"

He listened patiently as Sonya told him about the state of her family's financial affairs. He'd never met her aunt Nelda, and while she sounded like a pleasant woman, he wondered why she hadn't insisted her brother give Sonya power of attorney.

After hearing all the sordid details about her father's gambling problems, he wasn't surprised when she uttered the nightmare of all words for a homeowner, besides flood, fire and earthquake.

"Foreclosure."

Sonya began to cry, and Trent sat back against the sofa cushions.

"Aunt Nelda told me about the jewelry store. She told me she tried to save it, because she and my father had worked side by side to run the place for all those years. She thought she'd be able to take it over and run it herself. But my father was in too deep."

She nestled against his chest while he stroked her curls. He couldn't remember a time when he'd held a woman in his arms when she was upset. He never got involved deeply enough to allow a situation like that to happen, nor did he care to involve himself in their problems.

Sonya, on the other hand, was a woman he already respected. She was ambitious and independent, but not so much that she didn't need a shoulder to cry on every once in a while.

He gave her a kiss on the top of her head. "Why do

you think your aunt didn't tell you about the house? It seems like she would have had ample opportunity."

She dabbed at her eyes with her fingertips. "I didn't really let either of them know about my plans."

"Why was that? Were you having second thoughts about coming home?"

"I was confused about everything. I knew I wasn't happy dancing anymore, but for a long time, I thought it was because I was overly tired from my demanding performance schedule."

She sat up and grabbed a tissue from the end table, then proceeded to wipe her eyes. "By the time I'd decided, it was too late. My father had passed away."

"Oh, honey, I'm so sorry."

"It makes me wonder why am I even taking your class? Why should I bother, if we're going to lose the house anyway?"

He grinned. "So you can watch me put on a tool belt?"

She poked him in the side of his ribs with her elbow, and seemed to be a little more cheerful. "Would you be upset if I dropped your class?"

"Only if I couldn't see you again." His stomach growled loudly and Sonya giggled. "Why don't we continue this conversation in the kitchen? I have jerk chicken sandwiches and sweet potato fries in that sack."

He brought the plant with him and set it in the

middle of the table. "Welcome to your new home, little fella."

She took a couple of blue plates from the cupboard and handed them to him. "In case you haven't noticed, my thumb is not green. Does it require much care?"

"If you take care of it throughout the winter, you can plant it outside in the spring."

"I might not be here by then."

"You can come and live with me."

She gave him a deadpan look. "I'm serious, Trent."

"So am I, or I could build you the house of your dreams, if you'd let me."

"Thank you for the kind offer, Trent. But I'm going to stay right here as long as I can."

"Ever think about selling?"

"I grew up in this house. My relationship with my mother was good, but she passed away when I was very young. My father tried to pick up the slack, but he was very busy with the jewelry store. He didn't have much time for me, or for anyone else. My aunt did what she could, but I guess I grew up quickly, because I had no other choice. My father wanted me to be something I'm not. He wanted me to take over the jewelry store."

"My father wanted me to be like my brother, but I prefer to be outside slinging a hammer, no matter what the weather, than inside brokering land deals.

"Besides, selling this house is not my decision to make, but even if it was, I don't think I could do it."

"Why not?"

The low hum of the refrigerator was the only sound in the room, and it seemed as though his whole life was swinging on the hinge of her answer.

"Because of the memories we're making in it right now."

He gulped at the raw need in her eyes, and he understood, even before she said the words.

"I think I'm ready for that tour of the second floor. Are you?"

The stairs reacted noisily under their feet as they began to climb. It took all of Trent's concentration not to stare at Sonya's curves, and all of his efforts went south because he was hard all the same.

When they got almost all the way up, Sonya suddenly stopped and leaned against the faded blue-and-white-floral wallpaper.

Trent kept his eyes focused on her as she gripped the railing.

"I used to lie awake at nights, listening for my father's footsteps. Even when he was angry, he wasn't a door slammer. One thing I like about this home is that all the walls are made of plaster, so there's very good sound insulation. Often, the only way I knew he was home from the store was when the stairs creaked. Sometimes, he'd been here for hours. When I couldn't hear him, it was like he wasn't here at all."

She turned to face him. "I guess that pretty much sums up my relationship with my father."

He nodded and followed her the rest of the way. Her voice was quiet as she pointed out what had been her father's room and her aunt's room. Then came the small bathroom, and he told her that he wouldn't update a thing except the worn linoleum. He tried to push away the image of Sonya bathing in the claw-foot tub, letting all her troubles float away in the scented soapy water.

There was a small door next to the bathroom that led to the attic. He went up alone, noted the rusted red tricycle, a pink dollhouse with dusty green shutters and boxes of various shapes and sizes.

When he descended from the stairs, Sonya wasn't there, but he smelled a hint of smoke. Had she gone downstairs to light a fire in the fireplace? But he hadn't heard the stairs creak, so he walked to the only room that was left.

When he sauntered in, the first thing he saw was a stone fireplace. He hadn't realized she had one in her room. There were a couple of logs on the grate, just beginning to spark. But what he didn't see was Sonya.

"You should replace the insulation in the attic," he called out, unsure of where she was, or whether he should step farther into the room without her permission. "You'll stay warmer in the winter and save on your energy bill."

The embers were just beginning to spark. One popped, sending a small firework up the shaft, and he nearly jumped out of his shoes at the sound.

He took a chance and walked deeper into the room and was about to turn around when Sonya stepped out of a dressing alcove hidden behind the door.

"I think we can create our own heat right here, don't you think?"

His mouth fell open and he had to resist the urge to fall to his knees in front of her naked body.

"S-Sonya."

It had been a long time since he'd reacted so viscerally to a woman. The hard-on he had been nursing since he first comforted her in his arms became an uncomfortable arrow in his pants that needed relief soon.

His voice came out as a choked whisper, and he pressed his back against the door to close it. Arms at her sides, she came closer but he held out a hand to stop her.

She tilted her head, seeming confused, and a little part of his heart broke and hoped he hadn't hurt her by the gesture.

He held on to the crystal doorknob to steady himself.

"I just want to look at you. Please?"

She did not cross her arms in front of her chest, or hide herself from him in any way. In fact, he got the sense that she was opening herself up to him, even as he realized deep down that she was used to being stared at, and that made him sad in a way.

God, she was beautiful. He wanted to tell her, but he didn't want words to break through the lust that flowed through his veins. He'd never seen a woman so toned and lean, and yet so sensual.

"Baby, I'm going to cherish you."

The room was not cold by any means, and her nipples were dark flat nubs on perfectly shaped breasts. There was very little hair in the vee between her legs and he licked his lips in anticipation of the moisture he expected to find there.

He shed his clothes quickly, until he was exposed, too. Her eyes flitted down and took all of him in, her eyes roaming along his length so slowly, so carefully, that his mouth went dry for a moment.

His penis throbbed amid a bush of dark coarse hair he'd long ago stopped trimming. His balls ached and felt like they weighed a million tons.

He lifted his chin, and she smiled. Somehow, she knew that was her cue to come forward.

He ran a finger down the middle of her breasts, and she sighed. He flattened his palms and pressed them lightly against her nipples, and they came alive.

"What am I doing, Trent? Sometimes I don't know where to start, or how to begin."

Trent cupped one hand behind her neck, and lowered his mouth to hers. He was so close he could feel her breath on his lips.

"It begins with one kiss, and then, it's up to us."

"Show me, Trent," she whispered, closing her eyes.

The fire crackled in counterpoint to their elongated kisses as he encircled her waist with his hands, melding her to his body in a fluid dance that was only just beginning.

Chapter 7

Sonya held on tight as Trent walked them over to her bed. Her silk comforter felt like a cloud against her back as he gently laid her down. She stared boldly at the engorged length and girth of his masculinity, and felt an exquisite tug between her legs. He was perfect, and she could barely wait to feel him moving inside her.

She turned on her side and propped herself up on one elbow. She stroked the hair above his erect penis with her manicured fingertips. His abdomen caved in slightly at her touch.

"Are you trying to drive me crazy, Trent?" she cooed. "Because if you are, it's working."

Unable to stand it any longer, she flicked her tongue at his penis, but didn't make contact.

"You're teasing me," he groaned. "That's not fair."

He pushed her back gently on the bed, and her laughter morphed into low moans when he proceeded to lick each breast, one and then the other, until her nipples glistened.

"Are we going to have our first fight?"

He looked hurt. "Didn't you like it?"

"Oh, I loved it. I didn't want you to stop."

"Baby, I won't stop." He anchored her hips between his muscular thighs and bent over her body. Keeping his eyes on hers, he cupped his hands around her breasts, and she felt her mouth begin to water in anticipation.

"Make sure I don't stop, okay? Keep me honest. Keep me pleasuring you."

Sonya held his gaze as he began to suck on her nipples, and his actions were made even hotter by the temptation of his hot flesh resting on her belly.

She wanted to open her legs to accept him, but he had them pinned between his. Giving him that level of control excited her, because she knew she could turn the tables on him at any time, and take control back.

"How am I doing, baby? Am I stopping yet? Do you want me to?"

"D-doing fine," she moaned as he licked the undersides of her breasts. His tongue was a hot flame that never left her skin.

"D-don't stop." The sounds of him suckling on her breasts made her juices flow, and the heat in her lower abdomen began to swirl.

She tried to spread her legs again, and she felt his penis throb against her.

"But you're fighting me, Sonya," he soothed and buried his face in her neck, nuzzling her there. "Stop fighting me, baby."

Sonya wanted to tell him that he was holding her in place, by the power of his muscular thighs. She tried to reach to touch his penis, but he held her arms at her sides and kissed her with even more passion than before.

When he lifted his mouth, she saw more than lust in his eyes: she saw a tenderness so real that it speared her heart. At that moment, she knew Trent was the one she'd been waiting for all her life.

He released her hips, then slid his body upon her and threaded his fingers through her hair. "I'll only let you fight me if we can take our time making up."

"It's a deal," she whispered. "Let's take as long as we want."

"Want?" he asked, bringing his mouth to hers. "I more than just want you, Sonya."

Their tongues intermingled briefly, his heart melding into hers. She spread her legs and wrapped them around his buttocks.

"Tell me, Trent. Whisper it in my ear, so I'll hear your words long after you're gone."

His mouth left her lips and settled at the tip of her earlobe, and the low vibrations of his voice made her tremble.

"I need you, Sonya. Like I've never needed any-one before," he breathed, his voice hoarse with de-sire as he prepared to enter her. "Can I prove it to you? Can I make love to you?"

Her eyes crinkled at the edges as she held back tears. He was so big and so deliciously long. He was all the man she'd ever wanted, and then some. She dug her heels into the mattress and spread her legs even wider.

They groaned together as his flesh entered hers, ever so slowly. It was as if they both wanted to pre-serve the moment. She started to move her pelvis, but he stopped her with his hand, and pushed in a little more. Her thighs gripped his hips, and she steadied herself as he plunged into her fully.

Their eyes met and he braced both hands, palms flat on the mattress.

When he started to rhythmically move inside her, she closed her eyes and saw stars. His flesh bobbed against hers as he entered her again and again. She dug her heels into the mattress and swirled her pel-vis against his, as they challenged each other. Their movements grew more frantic with every thrust, punctuated by his sharp grunts. Her fingernails pressed into his clenched muscular buttocks, and she held on to him as the first orgasm rolled through her body.

He kept moving and moving, beads of sweat gathered in the small of his back, as the scent of their intense lovemaking filled the air between them.

She opened her legs even farther apart, and he rested his body upon hers and slowed his movements until he stilled.

Breathing heavily, he withdrew almost fully and then plunged back into her body again, and grunted out her name as they climaxed together. A long time later, when their hearts had stopped pounding and their breathing was calmer, he fell back into the pillows and cradled her in his arms.

"I'm not tired yet," she announced.

He laughed, and then saw the serious look on her face.

"You're serious, aren't you?"

She nodded and tucked her chin to his chest for a quick look at his current state.

"Oh, baby, that was a total knockout." He laughed, idly playing with her hair. "I don't know how I'll go another round."

"Don't worry, Trent. I've got just the cure."

Before he could protest, she enclosed her hand around his slippery penis, wet with her juices, made a tight seal and ever so slowly brought him back to life.

* * *

The next morning, Sonya yawned and stretched her aching muscles. A shiver of delight traveled up her body, from head to toe as she recalled the pleasure of Trent's tongue slowly licking her flesh in her most intimate areas.

The fire had burnt down to embers, but she was still glowing red hot for the man who'd pleasured her long into the night. For the first time since she'd been home, she did not have a pit of loneliness in her stomach, and it was a wonderful feeling. She was falling in love.

"Trent, are you still here?"

The house had settled into a solitary silence, but not the lonely kind. With Trent in her life, she would never be alone again.

She glanced over at her alarm clock, and saw it was 9:00 a.m. She was usually up by five, and in the dance studio by six. Even though she wasn't dancing, old habits died hard.

She'd overslept, and it was the best feeling ever.

The truth was she'd been craving a relationship for some time now, one where she was as invested in it as much as her partner. It hadn't been that way with her ex. She'd never had any time for him. Between dancing, lessons and performances, and healing between performances, there was never any time just for her, let alone a man.

Trent entered the room, breakfast tray in hand and a smile on his face.

"Is it morning already?"

She flopped back onto the pillows. "That was one night I wish had never ended."

"My lady was pleased?" He set the tray on the bed and gave her a chaste kiss on the forehead.

Sonya cupped his face between her hands and gave him a passionate kiss. "More than pleased. Couldn't you tell?"

"Hmm… Good thing you don't have any neighbors close by." He ran his hand up her thigh and she felt the heat of his skin through the blankets. "Should we skip breakfast?"

She sniffed the delicious aromas and patted his cheek. "Sorry, darling, but nothing gets between me and my bacon."

"I feel the same way about my first cup of coffee," he tossed back. "I'll put another log on the fire, and let's see if we can make it through breakfast, without tearing each other's clothes off."

He slipped her silk kimono robe on to her body. She turned around and as he tied the sash around her waist, she trembled at his touch.

"What's wrong?"

"Was last night as incredible as I remember?"

"It certainly was, and don't worry, we'll have lots more nights together."

"Will we?"

"Why do you doubt me?"

"Not you, me. All I know is the stage and preparing to perform on it. It's been a while since I've had a normal life and a normal relationship." She glanced around the room, and then at him. "This is like a whole different world."

He reached out and cupped her cheek. "I know it must be a difficult transition, but as I said last night, we can go as slow as you want. I'm here for you, Sonya."

She gave him a kiss that was slow and sweet. It was too soon to talk about the pace of their relationship, but she was glad that his words were not just pillow talk.

He poured her a cup of coffee, and then one for himself. "How did you get interested in dance, anyway?"

"My mother was a former dancer. She was born in Brooklyn and dreamed of being a Radio City Rockette.

"Unfortunately, her cup size was just a shade too small, her hips were just a smidge to wide and she was African-American, so she didn't make it."

She rose, went to her closet and pulled out a medium-sized paper box. There was a black-and-white picture of her mother when she was a teenager.

"Wow, she's beautiful. You look just like her."

"I found this box a few days ago in the attic. I

haven't had a chance to go through them. There are lots of newspaper and magazine clippings of me."

"Who kept all these? Your aunt?"

"Actually, it was my father. Nelda is the least sentimental person I've ever known. I was so shocked that I sat down on the attic floor and cried."

"This proves that he cared what happened to you, even after you two had a falling-out."

"Does it? Maybe he just kept hoping that I would eventually fail."

"Do you really believe that?"

"Yes, but I don't want to. I really want to believe that he only wanted the best for me, even if it wasn't exactly what he had planned for my future. I wish I could say that I would do things differently, in order to have a better relationship with my father, but I wouldn't."

She hid her face in her hands and for the first time in a long time, she didn't want to cry when she thought about her dad.

"He never understood that I had to find my way to the stage. I had to dance, or else my heart would have crumpled up and died."

Trent gently took her hands in his. "I'm sure, if we're ever blessed enough to be parents, that we'll make a lot of mistakes raising our children, too. I think the important thing is to learn from them and move on."

Sonya felt her heart beat faster and she told herself that he was probably just speaking rhetorically, not necessarily indicating that he wanted to have kids with her. Still, she was glad that he was open to being a father someday.

She slowly untied her kimono and let it fall off her shoulders. "I don't want to talk about the past, or the future. I want to act on the now."

She gave him a lingering kiss, and then reached down for his boxers. He slipped them off quickly, and his penis was already hard, thick and throbbing for action.

"What do you want to do?" he asked.

The desire in his eyes as he watched her crawl onto his lap made her even hungrier. She sat on her haunches and positioned herself over him. Her outer loins, already slick and moist, were ready as she clutched his thick shaft in her hand.

Their eyes met and she held on to his shoulders as her flesh slid all the way down his length, gripping him inside her. He uttered a long satisfying groan that roiled into her ears and made her swell with anticipation.

"Take me for a ride," she begged into his ear. "I want to go for a ride, Trent," she whispered.

Pelvis to pelvis, his thick flesh filled her up so much that she thought she might burst. She bit her lip and started to move with urgency, and he stopped her.

"Closer," he muttered and squeezed her buttocks,

inching her forward until there was no space between them.

"Now, slower, baby," he commanded, guiding her hips in a circular motion. "Let's make it last."

She moaned, tilting her head to the side as she moved up and down, while he controlled the speed of her hips, with his hands around her waist.

He trailed kisses down her exposed neck, and then moved back to her lips and enjoyed teasing her there, with his tongue in the deepest recesses of her mouth.

"Go ahead, baby." He cradled his hands behind her back to taste and suck her nipples, pressing her even closer to him. "Ride."

She braced her hands on Trent's shoulders and whimpered from the pleasure of his throbbing flesh and hot tongue as they moved together, one body, one heart.

Trent shielded his eyes from the bright morning sun as he walked toward a two-story sprawling structure, which right now was just two-by-fours but would soon be somebody's dream home.

His current development, Paradise Valley, which wasn't on a valley at all but on the edge of an eighteen-hole golf course, was 90 percent leased. The pressure was on from both his mother (who'd named it) and his customers to complete the rest of the homes sooner rather than later. His father had complete faith that he'd get it done, while Steve, who rarely visited the construction sites, relied on the weekly staff meetings for his updates.

It was slated to be a normal day of meeting with workers at each of the houses under construction, checking materials and pounding a few nails himself, if he got lucky.

Since entering into a relationship with Sonya, he couldn't get her off his mind. Their night of lovemaking had been exciting and eye opening. He never knew a woman that was more giving of pleasure than Sonya. She seemed to invoke a fire of lust and longing for her that he knew would be difficult to break.

He thought about the ties she had to her home. Why she was even considering living in an old-fashioned farmhouse, he couldn't understand, but he guessed when someone came back from being away for a while, it was nice to have a home to come back to, even if the memories there were not what you'd expected.

After he was done with this development, hopefully, it would be time to break ground on the affordable housing project.

He'd gone to his parents' house for dinner a few days ago, and his mother had taken him aside and flat out asked him when they were breaking ground. Although acquisition of land could take months, even years, some of the leads he'd given Steve were extremely viable.

Steve had not given Agnes an update in several

weeks, and he'd been mum at the status meetings. She needed to know if she had to start thinking about hiring workers and drafting press releases.

Agnes must have conveniently forgotten that her eldest son was a secretive man. Trent wasn't surprised that Steve had kept the details to himself. That was the way he worked, preferring to let the rest of the family know about his decisions well after he'd made them.

Sometimes, Steve discussed his plans with his father, but since he was Chief Financial Officer, his parents trusted him. So far, Steve hadn't been wrong and had made them all a lot of money.

Trent sighed as he unrolled a blueprint on the hood of his pickup. He placed a brick on each corner and radioed for his foreman. While he waited for the man to arrive, he leaned against his pickup truck and poured himself a steaming cup of coffee from his thermos.

He'd stayed in Bay Point his entire life, and sometimes he wondered why he did. The more houses he built here, the more he anchored himself to the community.

A short time later, he was reviewing the blueprints with a couple of his electricians when he heard a couple of horn honks. He glanced behind his shoulder and saw Steve waving from the window of his silver BMW.

Trent was determined to make Steve's exit as

quick and painless as possible. He loved his brother, but he did not belong here, and they both knew it.

He got out of the car and closed the door.

"Good morning. You have to be on your way to the detail shop, not coming from, right?"

Because not all the homes were complete, the street had not been paved yet. Steve hated his vehicles to be dirty.

"I'm here because I have a very important question."

"I'm not hiring," he joked.

"Ha ha." Steve replied. "I have a lead on some property for the affordable housing project. But first, I need to know if you're hooking up with that hot dancer who's new in town."

Steve's tone implied that Sonya was a stripper.

Trent clenched his fist and wanted to level him with a one-punch, but he held back. Because of his brother, Sonya probably already had a negative impression of the Waterson family. He didn't need to add to it.

"She's a ballerina. Stop trying to insinuate that she's something else."

Steve guffawed. "Her father was a broken-down gambler. What else am I supposed to think?"

Before Trent knew what was happening, his fist was gripping Steve's collar.

Steve furrowed his brow in shock. "Jeez, man, calm down. What's wrong with you? I know we've had our scrapes, but we're not twelve years old any-more."

"I know that, but do you?" Trent demanded, and shook his brother once more. "Do you?"

"Yeah, just let me go, okay?"

Trent paused, and then without warning, thrust his fist forward and opened his hand.

Steve stumbled backward. He almost tripped and fell on a short stack of wood.

"I'm sorry. I don't know what came over me."

Except Trent did know. It was Sonya. He was fall-ing in love with her, and he felt an overwhelming need to protect her. Plus, all the expectations, spo-ken and unspoken, that went along with it.

Except tying the knot, and he breathed an inward sigh of relief. Clearly, she wasn't marriage-minded; she'd left a guy in San Francisco who had wanted to take her to the altar.

Wait a minute, he told himself as his mind spun over the words. Was he falling for Sonya?

He already had, he decided, even before their bod-ies moved together in passion through the night.

He knew now that there was no specific sign that he was in love with Sonya. He always had been. He'd just needed to meet her to make his dream of the per-fect woman come true.

Steve straightened his collar and fixed his shirt where it had become untucked. "It's okay. We're both under a lot of pressure right now. Dad is on me about this affordable housing project."

"Have you found any suitable land yet?"

"Funny you should ask. How deep are you in with this woman?" Steve asked.

Suspicion pricked at his brain. "Her name is Sonya."

"Well, I met a lady in line at that hamburger shop."

"You're losing your touch, Steve."

Steve frowned. "She was about sixty and not my type. Anyway, I overheard her talking about her niece named Sonya, and I think it might be the same girl."

Trent arched a brow. "It might be, why?"

"She was talking about Sonya and said that she was going to be selling the home and the land with it. And when she mentioned the amount of acreage— eight hundred acres!—I nearly offered to pay for her lunch."

He paused and gave an apologetic shrug. He had a feeling his brother was trying to elicit information.

"But I couldn't, because then they'd have known I was listening in on their conversation."

Trent didn't say anything and went around to grab another mechanical pencil from his glove compartment.

"What about it, bro? Is she willing to sell? I'm not too familiar with that area, but I looked it up on a satellite map. That's prime land! Maybe not for the affordable housing project—no, it's too good for that, but for our custom developments, it's quite a find."

"Don't even think about it," Trent warned, not bothering to inform Steve that the house and land now belonged to Sonya's aunt. "It's not for sale."

"How do you know?" Steve pressed on. "Did you ask her, or were you too busy ridin'?"

"None of your business to both of your questions. This discussion is over. What about the leads I gave you a couple of weeks ago?"

"None of them panned out," Steve muttered.

Trent got the sense that he hadn't even followed up on them. His brother was never keen on accepting help doing his job from anyone, but especially from Trent.

"Are you sure she won't sell? I got kind of a way with women."

Trent held in a laugh. His brother's arrogance was too much. "Go back to the office, Steve. You're out of your element here."

Trent waited until Steve was gone, and then he rolled out another blueprint. It wasn't long before he was having difficulty keeping his mind on the drawings. He kept seeing Sonya, in his arms, in the nude, and it took everything in his power not to hop in his truck and drive over to her place.

"Snap out of it, Waterson," he muttered to himself. Deep down, he knew that was going to be impossible. Not only did he want Sonya, he was falling in love with her.

Chapter 8

Sonya looked in the full-length mirror and held up a purple-and-black-leopard-spotted bra and panty set over her gray yoga pants and white tank top. She compared it with one that was made of the most delicate cream-colored French lace she'd ever seen.

She bit her lip, truly conflicted. To really get a feel for the look, she'd have to strip down to her skivvies, but she hated dressing rooms.

The boutique lingerie shop was the newest addition to downtown Bay Point's growing cadre of small business retailers, and was crowded with shoppers. Sonya had stopped in to get something special for an upcoming date she had with Trent. He wouldn't tell her where they were going, other than to wear something sexy.

After a few minutes of indecision, she shrugged and grinned at her reflection. "Guess I'll just have to purchase both!" she said aloud.

Sonya heard a raucous "Go for it, honey!" from a female voice nearby. She turned around and it was Violet, the woman from the home repair class.

"Hey, girl, where have you been?" Violet squealed, causing a few heads to turn around. She set down two shopping bags on the polished wood floor. "I must have been in the line to pay when you walked in or else I would have seen you."

The two women hugged tight, like they were fierce friends, and Sonya felt a twinge of guilt for not keeping in contact. The last time she'd seen Violet was at Sal's Hardware store.

After releasing one other, Violet teased, "Or maybe should I ask, who have you been with?"

Sonya swung the two sets of lingerie in the crook of her index finger. "I've been a little busy."

Violet raised a brow and laughed. "I'll bet, and about to get busier, I imagine."

Sonya merely smiled, neither confirming nor denying that she was in a relationship. She wasn't even sure that Trent wanted anyone to know. Maybe he had his own reasons for staying mum, and that was fine with her. For now.

Violet folded her arms. "So are you going to tell me who the lucky man is?"

She pressed her lips together and shook her head.

"I can't, Violet. I'm sorry."

Violet shrugged, and gave her a knowing smile.

"I think I know who it is. You haven't been in class lately, and I've had him all to myself."

Sonya felt her face get hot. Although news would break at some point that she and Trent were dating, she wasn't going to be the one to spill the information and spoil the secrecy.

Violet winked. "And I'm not talking about the power saw."

Sonya burst out laughing. She'd forgotten how humorous Violet could be. "I certainly hope not, Violet. I wouldn't want you to get hurt."

"And I don't want you to get hurt," Violet added in a serious tone. She picked up her shopping bags, looked around at the crowd and edged closer.

"Can I talk to you outside?"

"Sure, just let me pay for these purchases."

A few minutes later, Sonya joined her and they walked to the town square, where an old-fashioned carousel was the main attraction. They each bought homemade lemonade from a sidewalk vendor and then settled back on a worn park bench.

Sonya took a sip of her drink first and scrunched up her face. "Oh, my, that is sour. Go easy."

Violet grinned and raised hers. "That's exactly what I wanted to talk to you about."

She tilted her head. "Fresh-squeezed lemons?"

"No, men who look sweet on the outside, but can make vinegar out of your heart."

"And who do you think is going to do that to me?"

"I think we both know who, Sonya. Remember what I said to you that first day in class? Trent Waterson is a heartbreaker. Remember that?"

She nodded gravely. "Yes, of course I do. And I appreciate your advice. I just haven't seen any inclination that Trent would do that to me."

Violet gasped. "So my suspicions were right, you and Trent are dating!"

Sonya grabbed Violet's wrist. "Don't tell anyone, okay? I'm so happy. I really am."

"Enjoy it while you can get it. He's a heartbreaker," Violet repeated matter-of-factly. "Plain and simple."

Sonya put her hands on her hips. "Why don't you tell me why he has this reputation?"

"About a year ago, his brother's girlfriend tried to seduce him. But according to her, he wasn't interested. Then when she tried to go back to Steve, he didn't want her, either. It caused a real rift between them. That's why I call him a heartbreaker."

"Do you know how ridiculous that sounds?"

"Ask the girl who this happened to if she thinks this behavior sounds crazy."

Sonya studied her friend, and became aware that it was Violet who had had her heart broken by the Waterson men.

"I'm sorry, Violet. I didn't mean to sound so unfeeling."

She waved her comment away and slumped against the bench.

"No, I'm the one who should be sorry. I shouldn't let my negative experiences influence you. We're two very different women with one thing in common. We both think Trent Waterson is the hottest man in a tool belt."

The two women, relieved the tension was broken, were consumed by laughter. They took long drags on their lemonades to try and calm down. But each time they did, the pinched looks on their faces from the tart drinks made them roll again.

"Both the Waterson men are extremely wealthy, but Trent hasn't allowed money and success to change him."

Violet draped her arm on the park bench and turned reflective.

"Maybe that's why I was attracted to him. Steve and I dated for over a year. He never treated me badly, not exactly. He just didn't act like I was his everything. He cared more about making the next real-estate deal than spending time with me."

Sonya rattled the ice in her cup and confided, "I think I'm falling in love with Trent."

She told Violet about the rose plant that he'd bought her and all the other little gifts in the weeks since then. There was a diamond ankle bracelet, a pair of gold earrings, a bouquet of flowers and a gift certificate for a day spa.

"He cares about me," she affirmed, finally believing it in her heart.

Violet nodded. "I wouldn't doubt it. Trent is a nice guy. He told me that he would never date another man's woman, especially his brother's. He told me to go back to Steve, but even when I explained that nothing happened between us, he was so hurt that I even flirted with Trent that he never spoke to me again."

"Good riddance," Sonya said. "A guy who can't forgive is a man a woman should forget."

"Yeah. The funny thing is, I didn't even take the class to make Steve jealous. I took it because I'm actually interested in home repair."

"You didn't know Steve was supposed to teach the class? Trent only stepped in because Steve asked him to at the last minute."

Violet dropped her empty cup. Half-melted ice cubes spilled on the ground. "You're kidding!" She snorted. "He gets hives if the sink gets stopped up. He must have been signed up to teach just to meet girls. He probably saw me on the class list and panicked."

The two women enjoyed another good laugh, and

then made sure they had each other's contact information.

"I've got an appointment at the salon, so I'd better go." Violet primped her short bob and grinned. "You never know, the love of my life may be just around the corner. Keep in touch, girl. I'm expecting a gold-embossed invite to the wedding real soon."

Sonya waved goodbye and headed toward the side street where her car was parked.

Deep down, she knew that she and Trent were building something special, something real. But marriage? She thought about how her father had insisted her mother put his needs ahead of her own. How she had slowly folded into herself, wallowing in a misery that weakened her immune system. The doctors could never explain the sudden onset of ovarian cancer, but even at a young age, Sonya knew her mother had simply given up.

She and Trent enjoyed a sweet give and take in their relationship that was wholly satisfying; but how long would it last? He claimed he didn't get involved in the business side of things, but men could be very fickle. How long before she was no longer a priority and he put his business ambitions first?

Trent draped his arm around Sonya and gave a victory yell.

They'd had breakfast together and then hopped in his truck and drove to Estela Bay, located about one hundred miles from Bay Point. The cliff was accessible only by steep hiking trails. But when they made it to the top and emerged from the tall grasses that flanked them on either side, the view of the Pacific Ocean was spectacular.

"It's gorgeous," Sonya said. "I just wish the sun would come out."

A mantle of dark clouds overhead threatened rain, and the picnic lunch they'd brought along.

He took her in his arms. "Oh, I don't care. Let it pour. The rain is what brought us together."

"Are you trying to be romantic again?"

"Oh, you're talking about the hiking boots? They weren't romantic enough, huh?"

She thought a moment. "It certainly wasn't what I expected. I mean, when you said to dress up, I thought—"

He did a little twirl and took a bow. "I was taking you dancing. That was a beautiful gown you had on, but I had fun taking you out of it."

She laughed. "We almost didn't get out of the house on time, let alone eat breakfast."

"But we did, because we're a team."

He looped his arm through hers, beat his chest with his other hand and bellowed, "And we're ready to conquer the world!"

"You're silly," she said, laughing. "Must be the altitude."

"I'm serious, baby. There's beauty in the rainstorms of life. You and I are living proof."

He stuck one leg out in the air and waved it around. "Plus our matching hiking boots are pretty darn cool."

She set the picnic basket down on the grass and opened it. "Maybe we better eat before you start quoting sonnets."

He grinned and spied the picnic basket that he'd had catered especially for them. There was a selection of assorted sandwiches, fruit salad, fresh brownies and sparkling water.

"I guess you're right. No more wowing you with my romanticisms. I vote for lunch."

He helped her spread out the red-plaid blanket, and then they sat down. While Sonya set everything out, Trent navigated to his music app on this phone and turned on his small Bluetooth speaker.

He raised his bottle of water and clinked it with hers. "Bon appétit!"

They opened their sandwiches and ate silently.

Trent was thankful that Sonya wasn't the type of woman who talked incessantly. She seemed content to let conversation ebb and flow naturally, and if there were gaps, it didn't mean their mutual interest was waning. Even better, she didn't act bored when he talked about his job, and when he told her that his wealth kept him grounded, she completely understood and seemed almost thankful.

He never knew Sonya's father, but he felt sorry for the man who had squandered most of his hard-earned wealth away through his addiction to gambling so there was nothing left for his only daughter.

He had more than enough money that if he ever wanted to walk away from Waterson Builders and start his own company, he could. But he was committed to supporting his family's vision, and he had his future to think about, too. One that he hoped would include Sonya, if she were willing.

"I'd love to show you my home someday. I've got a gourmet kitchen that I rarely get to use. You and I could make some mean PB&Js in there."

"That's one thing we have in common—neither of us enjoy cooking."

"But it would be so much fun to learn."

She put down her sandwich and replied quietly, "I'm going to ask you a question, and don't take it the wrong way, okay?"

He felt his heart drop. "I'll try. What is it?"

"Do you think we're seeing too much of each other?"

He set down his sandwich, no longer hungry due to the tone of concern in her voice. "No, as a matter of fact, I wish I could see you more often."

"When I officially open the studio, my time will be more limited."

"I realize that, and I'll adjust. I know it's tough starting a new business."

She nodded and lowered her voice. "Thank you. It's just that I feel like things are moving too quickly sometimes. I don't want you to be disappointed."

A trickle of fear crept up his spine. Trent wasn't afraid of much, except losing Sonya.

He cupped her chin and looked deeply in her eyes. "I could never be disappointed by you." When she moved away, he asked, "What brought about this concern?"

Tears came to her eyes. "I guess I'm just afraid of what's next. There are so many unknowns, with regards to my studio. Will I get enough students? Will they like me? Can I handle the parents? And most of all, can I teach what I know about ballet effectively?"

Trent pulled her into a hug. "You will be successful, and you know why? Because you love what you do. When my brother dropped the home repair class in my lap, I have to admit, I was scared. I wondered if I could do it. But it's actually been really easy and fun."

Sonya sniffed. "Have the women been concentrating on the lesson or have they been distracted by your tool belt?"

He shrugged, but was secretly pleased at the hint of jealousy in her voice. "Do you want me to ask them? Maybe do an in-class survey?"

She slapped his thigh lightly. "Of course not, although, it might be already around town that we're dating."

"How do you know?"

"I ran into Violet while shopping at that new lingerie shop in town." She put her hands over her mouth. "I wasn't supposed to tell you."

He tapped his chin with his index finger. "Come to think of it, Violet's seductive glances toward me have drastically reduced. I was feeling unlusted, but I guess that explains it. She must know I'm yours."

He cradled her face in his hands. "And I want the whole world to know you're mine."

They shared a tender kiss as the Pacific Ocean tumbled far below them. He wished he could make love to her on the beach, but unfortunately there was no access.

He stood up and reached for her hand, and when she was near him, he pointed up the coast.

"See that house?"

The sun had broken through the clouds, and Sonya shaded her eyes. "That one, way down there? The one that looks like its hanging off the cliff?"

He laughed. "Yes, it's only an optical illusion, but that's where we are headed after our picnic. We've got the whole place to ourselves."

She threw her arms around his neck. "Can we go now?"

He was relieved at the desire in her eyes. "No more talk about us seeing each other too much, promise?"

Sonya gave him a quick kiss and they cleaned

up their picnic odds and ends. Once the basket was packed, they set off back to his truck.

The house was a five-minute drive from the cliffs, and when they arrived, Trent glanced over at Sonya for her reaction.

Judging from the smile on her lips and her wide eyes, she was pleased with the arrangements. "Honey, all this is for us? It's gorgeous."

Trent got out of the car. "Three bedrooms and two baths of fun and seclusion."

He joined Sonya, who was still gazing at the dwelling. It pleased him that she seemed to like it so much.

"There are so many windows," she said in an awed tone. "And there's a solar panel on the roof."

"Yes, but note all the trees surrounding us. There's plenty of shade on the home. That panel provides much of the power.

"This is one of our concept homes. It was actually designed by Liza. My family loved it so much, we decided to furnish it for seasonal rentals rather than sell it outright."

"That's a great idea. I can't wait to see inside."

"I thought you'd never ask." He grabbed their overnight bags from the back seat. "Let's go!"

They entered the home, and he stowed their bags next to the grand stairwell that led to the second floor. Sonya slipped out of her hiking boots and headed toward the great room.

He did the same and followed her. "What do you think?"

She went on tiptoe and twirled around in her socks. "This is the most beautiful space I've ever seen."

The large room was glassed-in on all sides, except for the roof. Tall sycamore trees provided shade from the midafternoon sun.

"Wait till you see this."

He grabbed her hand, opened the patio door and led her out onto the deck. "The view of the ocean is even more magnificent. Just don't look down," he warned. "Remember the cliff?"

But Sonya did anyway and swooned into his arms. He caught her easily.

"I gotcha," he said, holding on to her waist tightly. If he had a choice, he'd never let her go.

"I swear, I'm not afraid of heights," she assured him. "I once flew over the audience's heads during a performance."

He stroked his fingers through her curly hair. "This is where you belong. Here with me. I want to protect you. From whatever and whomever frightens you."

She tilted her chin and stared into his eyes. "What if what I'm most afraid of is us?"

He placed his hands gently on her shoulders. "Whatever it is that we feel for one another, we can handle it. Just as long as we are honest with ourselves and each other."

She gave him a shy smile. "I'm kind of glad for rainstorms."

"Me, too." He caressed her hair. "How about a tour of the second floor?"

"I'd love it."

He swooped her up in his arms, and after sliding the patio door shut, carried her upstairs. He didn't stop moving until he reached the master bedroom.

The ocean-view room had many windows with sheer drapes held back by large gold tassels. The queen bed, modern in its circular design, blossomed with lots of cream-colored pillows and a luxurious dark blue duvet with gold piping.

As soon as she was on her feet, Sonya began unbuttoning his shirt. If she wanted him naked first, he was happy to oblige.

He let his arms hang at his sides. Her fingers worked quickly, almost feverishly. As every button was loosed, she planted a kiss on his skin.

Finally, his shirt fell to the floor, and he kicked it out of the way.

She took a step back and admired him. Her smile was a bit devious, like someone who was about to indulge in something a little naughty. It made him harden even more than he already was.

Sonya stepped toward him and placed her hands on his chest. His muscles twitched involuntarily when she moved her palms lightly over his nipples. They budded up, and he gasped at how her movements upon his sensitive skin had caused such an immediate reaction.

"Do that again, baby."

She did as he commanded, and when she was done, licked each tender bud just once. The sensation from her tongue traveled all the way down to his knees.

He fell in front of her and buried his face between her thighs. Her scent was muted through her clothes but he wanted to wait for her signal to remove them from her body.

What he couldn't wait for was to kiss her there. It was one of his favorite places on her body to pleasure her.

Without warning, he pressed his lips just under where her zipper began. The fabric was already a little moist, and he enjoyed the moan that poured from her lips.

She stroked one finger alongside his jaw, and his eyes followed her movements when she slipped it inside her shorts, loose at the waist, and touched herself there.

Trent felt he was almost going to burst as he watched her finger move inside the fabric, to places he couldn't get at yet, for what seemed like forever. He worked his lips expectantly, until her finger emerged, glistening with her juices, which he promptly licked clean.

She leaned down and kissed him, sharing in her taste.

"Want more?" she asked, and he didn't even have to nod, before she performed the same movements.

He remained kneeled before her, mesmerized by her hips swaying enticingly before his eyes. She stroked his face, then herself, gave him a taste of her wetness and captured his mouth in a blistering kiss.

He was in a daze, just watching her pleasure herself; the next thing he knew, he was unbuttoning her shorts.

She didn't put out a hand or tell him to stop, so he let them fall to the floor. He hooked his thumbs on her panties and shoved them down.

He sat back on his haunches, and took a moment to admire her femininity, before placing his hands on her bare bottom. He edged her closer to him, until her toes touched his knees. With his fingers, he gently spread her outer lips, plump and slick.

Trent tried to swallow his desire, but all he wanted to do was to devour her flesh, as slow and as long as she could take it. He let go of her buttocks and with his fingers found her most sensitive part.

He touched the tip of his tongue there, and she crumpled over him, making him lose contact. He slid his lips over her flat abdomen and clutched her ass to keep her near him. She moaned his name and straightened, clapping her hands on either side of his head. Quickly, his tongue darted and probed, licking her everywhere that was moist.

After a while, she cried out as her body started to convulse, and she fell to her knees on the carpet. He caught her and laid her down gently. Her legs fell open and he dove in and licked her insides until her hips began bucking uncontrollably.

"Hold on, baby," he gasped.

Trent swore as he tore off his clothes, almost losing his seed in the process.

Now completely nude, he swiftly penetrated her and ground out her name as he began to thrust inside her.

"Sonya, Sonya."

He took it slow at first—pumping, pumping. He watched as she threaded her fingers through her hair, elbows perpendicular to the ceiling.

"Sonya, Sonya."

Her upper half was still clothed, and he could see the edges of her nipples poke at the fabric of her T-shirt as she writhed on the floor.

He bit each one lightly with the edge of his teeth, never stopping his movements below, and she murmured his name in response.

Her body held him in a vise he never wanted to escape and she gave him free rein to pleasure them both.

When her moans turned to high-pitched mewls, he knew she was almost there.

"I love you, Sonya," he gasped and thrust into her one final time. "I love you so much."

She hitched in a breath at his words and clamped her legs around him tight, and the world stopped spinning for a moment. He captured her lips in a kiss, and their tongues devoured each other as they exploded together in sensual agony.

When their breathing slowed and heart rates returned to normal, Trent picked Sonya up in his arms and laid her on the bed. She felt heavier than before, and he knew it was because she was exhausted, and so was he.

Although the sex was incredible, it bothered him that she had not responded to his profession of love. He felt a pain in his heart that should not have been there. *Did she even hear him?* He didn't regret the words at all, but now he wondered if she felt the same way.

He gazed into her eyes and he saw that they were moist.

"Trent?" she muttered weakly. "I-I'm sorry."

He knew why she was apologizing, but he didn't want to discuss it right now. If she didn't love him, he didn't even want to think about what that might mean.

He smoothed her hair back from her forehead. "There's nothing to be sorry for," he soothed. "I'm going to run us a bath."

He started the water in the jetted tub, poured in some soap bubbles and checked the temperature. Then he stood in front of the toilet to take a leak. It was a long time before he could go, his body still calming down from their lovemaking. He washed his hands and face, turned off the water.

Sonya took her turn, and when she called him back in, she was already lounging in the tub.

At the sight of her wet, soapy body, he hardened again and she smiled.

He'd never wanted a woman this much before in his life.

So much for a rest, he mused, and quickly got in.

She'd pinned up her hair, and he longed to tug it loose, but he knew she'd probably get mad.

When he eased in next to her, to his surprise, she stood up and straddled his legs. Droplets of water beaded and dripped down her breasts and onto his face before she slowly descended without saying a word.

He sucked in a deep breath when she slid his penis inside her. She was even hotter than before. Yet, she still didn't speak.

He grabbed hold of her breasts, and Sonya began to swivel her hips. She felt so good, and he wanted to continue, but something wasn't right.

He moved away from her, and slid out of her body, feeling more alone than ever.

"What's wrong, Sonya?"

"Nothing," she insisted and brushed her lips teasingly against his.

She seemed determined to have him. One of her hands searched underwater and began to play.

"Is there only one participant in this party?" she inquired with a demure smile.

His body, defying his wishes, still wanted her. He wanted to succumb to her again, despite the fact that she'd rejected him.

He brought her hand out from under the water. "Not now. Not until you tell me what's wrong."

"I just want to show you that I care about you. Even if I can't say the same words that you said to me."

The water hissed and swirled around their bodies as Trent thought about what he would say.

"I always wondered why I never told a woman that I loved her first. Now I know that it's because you're the first woman I've ever truly loved."

"You don't know what you're saying, Trent. You just got caught up in the heat of the moment, that's all."

"Why does me loving you scare you so much?"

"I don't know. Maybe because I'm starting to feel the same way, or maybe because I'm not. I guess I need time to sort out my feelings for you."

She trailed kisses up and down his neck, distracting him from the fact that she was slowly lowering her body onto his once more. Her insides were like a smoldering fire, enticing and warm.

His hands inched up her back, massaging her skin as he buried his face between her breasts, and she began to rock and sway. The water lapped at their bodies as they melded and moved together.

I love you, Sonya.

He wasn't sure if it was the steam from the bath or emotion in his heart, but tears came to his eyes. He wiped them away on her skin as he nuzzled against it. He'd never met a woman with a sex drive that even came close to his, and now he had. He couldn't turn away from loving her and caring about her, not when his whole soul was at stake.

"Please, Trent, give me time. I want you so much, and I want us both to be happy."

When he knew he could handle it without breaking down, he gazed into her eyes. He knew she was being sincere, despite her fear. He also knew that she was worth the wait, no matter how long it took.

Chapter 9

Sonya hummed as she swished a dust broom over the newly polished wood floor of her dance studio. There were a million things she'd rather do besides clean, but when she was done, she always felt a sense of satisfaction. Soon, Trent would arrive for a visit, and he would be the first person in the space, besides various contractors.

When she was done sweeping, she stowed the broom in the closet and glanced around with a sense of pride.

It really is a beautiful space.

She was glad she had been able to purchase the historic building downtown. The selling point was a series of windows that spanned the entire top half of the building with a beautiful view of the ocean.

Yet every time she thought about opening the doors to the public, she broke out in a cold sweat. Her plan was to offer lessons for children first, and then later on, adults.

She had fond memories of donning glittery costumes for the recitals her former teacher had had twice a year in the winter and the spring.

She was planning to do the same thing, and from her research, they were a lot more complicated to run than she'd imagined. She'd need an army of parents to volunteer, fund-raising and most importantly, a building with a stage.

She moved into a cross-legged position on the floor and brought her arm up and around her head and stretched.

Her body was tense from anxiety and lack of sleep. Last night, Nelda had called her to apologize again for not telling her the bad news. It would have been easy to stay angry, but it wouldn't have done any good, nor would it have changed the circumstances.

She'd nearly fainted when her aunt told her how much she owed the bank. She'd spent much of the night racking her brain, trying to figure out a way to get the cash. Short of taking out a loan, it was impossible.

The circumstances were dire, but Sonya believed

there was a greater purpose in everything good or bad that happened to her. If she hadn't come home to Bay Point, she wouldn't have met Trent. He was the kindest, sexiest and most thrilling man she had ever met. That was reason enough not to stay angry with her aunt.

She bent forward and stretched toward the mirror, as if she were trying to grab her life back with her hands.

Still, the situation she faced worried her. She didn't want to live in an apartment, luxury or otherwise. She wanted her own space, her home with room to roam. After the big-ticket items were taken care of, like the new roof and new windows that Trent had recommended, she planned to redecorate the family home, room by room.

As for the hundreds of acres of land, she had a wild idea of starting a winery. If she ever got tired of teaching dance, at least she'd have a fallback plan. She had no idea how many grapes it took to make wine, and with her limited funds, she would have to start small, but it made her less anxious to think about options for her future.

But her first priority was the house, and making it a sanctuary, for as long as she was blessed enough to live there.

In a way, it already was.

The memories she and Trent had created there over the past few months could last a long time, if she wanted. He would come over at least three times a week, after work, and spend most Saturdays with her. Sometimes, they would go for a drive along the coast, and stop for dinner at a romantic restaurant.

They'd spent hours talking with their arms entwined around one other. Though it was difficult at first, she found herself opening up to him more and more. He was so gentle with her, so patient, and it amazed them both that they'd never met before. But she supposed it was because they were part of two different social circles. His family was corporate, big business and her family was more mom-and-pop shop.

She and Trent were both hardworking and ambitious, but they also knew that downtime and relaxation were important. That was part of their common ground, not to mention their sexual attraction to each other. She just enjoyed being with him, no matter what they were doing.

Sonya stretched toward the window, bent over and touched her toes. "If we lose the house, I guess I could always squat here."

Even though she was extremely fond of Trent, he was one reason why she wasn't sure she could stay in Bay Point permanently. After he'd professed his love for her, she knew he had been very hurt when she couldn't say the words back. She didn't know why she'd fallen silent, and couldn't tell him how she felt.'

Her heart stirred whenever he looked at her,

kissed her, touched her. Maybe it was because sometimes she got the feeling that there was something he wasn't telling her.

She'd read in the newspapers that his family, though wealthy, weren't the most popular people in town. People who had lived in Bay Point since childhood had a hard time affording their homes. Most were sold to newcomers who had no prior connection to the town, and others to people who wanted a second home close to the ocean.

It was revealed that the home repair classes that Trent was teaching were a means to appease the negative sentiment. As far as she'd heard, it wasn't working.

What could he have to hide? she wondered.

Most humans didn't get through life without a little bit of dirty laundry. Trent had a habit of leaving his clothes on the floor, but he always picked them up when she reminded him. She only hoped that she could handle whatever secret he was holding inside.

Other than his attachment to his vintage motorcycle collection, Trent didn't seem to be overly materialistic. He was probably the most content, relaxed man she'd ever met. And she had the sense it wasn't because he never had to worry about money—it was just who he was.

She pushed her doubts away for the moment and braced her elbows on her knees. She ignored her reflection and concentrated on the long box that held the barres in front of her. It was the final and most important part of the studio, and she'd been trying to drum up the courage to get it installed for over a month.

Everything else was done. A long mirror opposite the windows had been installed, so that her students could monitor their ballet positions for accuracy. There were benches, lockers and mirrors in the changing room. She'd had the toilets replaced with ones that actually worked. The entire place had been painted.

She thought about her conversation with Trent, and how she'd revealed her fear that teaching would not be enough to fulfill her. Since leaving the professional dance world, the need to perform had not gone away like she'd thought it would. Her only comfort was that her feelings were not unusual. Professional athletes who tried to retire often took up a different sport, just to remain active and in the limelight.

Many times, she'd thought about confessing her feelings to her former colleagues. The ones who had begged her not to quit had remained her friends. Those who were silently applauding the prospect that her spot would open up, allowing them the chance to step into her place, were not.

Trent had listened and not judged her, and she valued his open perspective. He simply wanted her to be happy, no matter what she was doing.

She heard the roar of the motorcycle below and

went to the window. By now, she recognized the raucous sound, though she'd refused his many offers for another ride. He teased her constantly about it, but she didn't mind. She enjoyed their easy banter, and would always tell him that she would join him again, someday. She never told him how hot it made her to watch him roll up to her house on his cycle.

From the doorway, she watched him bound up the stairs to her, toolbox in hand. Despite his heavy construction boots, there was a spring in his step and a smile on his face. He was like a kid coming home after being outside all day. She tried to tell herself that his joy was because of his work, but now she knew that it was because he loved her.

He loves me, and I love him. But she couldn't tell him. Not yet.

He put down the toolbox and tried to swoop her into his arms. She put her hands on his chest. "Not so fast, buddy. Those come off."

"The clothes?" he asked. "I don't have a problem with that." He started to unbutton his shirt, and she laughed, pointing to a long bench just inside the studio door.

"No, the shoes, silly. Socks or bare feet only on the studio floor."

He plopped down and removed the offenders, a sulk on his face that was well played. He reached for her hand and pulled her onto his lap. The passionate kiss he gave her was no act, and she felt it all the way to her toes.

In a way, she was relieved that he had even shown up. It meant that he was being true to his word, and giving her time to explore her own feelings about him and the future of their relationship.

He picked her up and walked into the studio, and the sight of the two of them in the mirror almost brought tears to her eyes. They looked like a couple of lovesick teenagers. She'd be a fool to let him go.

Her mouth sought his and she gave him a lingering kiss. When they parted, he let out a low whistle and she slid to the floor. Her legs felt like they were made of jelly.

"Thank you for coming here, Trent."

"No worries. I wish I could stay all day, but I've only got an hour before I have to be at the job site."

She pointed to the box on the floor. "The barres are in there, five of them. I hope the installers left room between each mirror.

Trent crouched down and opened the box. He pulled out the barres, plus all the associated hardware.

She watched as he stood up and measured the width of the mirror, and then did the same for the barres.

"We should be okay. I'll just power up my drill and have these installed in a jiffy."

She bit her lip and hoped he couldn't tell she was anxious about the installation.

He glanced over and gave her a quick hug. "Stop worrying, okay? Go do something and I'll call you when I'm done."

Sonya trudged into her little office. She reviewed proofs for her signage to the sound of Trent's drill. As much as she loved him in her home, she found that she didn't mind him in the studio, either. Again, he brought a sense of calm in the midst of her doubt and whirlwind emotions. She was starting to rely on him more and more, and that part frightened her.

She emailed her comments to the designer and then picked up her phone to call her aunt.

Her brow furrowed when there was no answer, so she left a voice mail for the second time that day.

Nelda had served as general manager and book-keeper at the jewelry store. Now that the store was closed, she kept busy volunteering for several non-profit organizations in town.

Although she'd sunk most of her savings into try-ing to save the store, her investments were sound and were being used for her living expenses. Sonya completely understood why she was resistant to liq-uidating those funds to pay off another set of her deceased brother's loans.

Sonya had visited a lawyer several days ago to see if there was anything she could do to save the family home. He'd confirmed that she could use the studio as collateral to save her home, but cautioned her about the risk. She knew her aunt would agree with the lawyer's warning.

The problem was that her aunt didn't know about the appointment, and now she felt guilty about it. She wanted to tell her right away, but she couldn't get her on the phone, and Nelda refused to text.

Trent appeared in the doorway. "All finished. Want to check it out?"

She popped out of her chair and walked into the studio. The barres were up and in perfect alignment with each other. The floor was free from drywall dust. Other than signage for the front door, everything on her list was done. She could open for business whenever she was ready.

Now, all she had to do was get past the fear that teaching would completely replace her need to perform, and she'd be all set.

"Great job, Trent. Thank you!"

He pulled her into his arms. "I'm glad you're happy. I strive to satisfy."

She gave him a hug. "And you do satisfy me, more than I could have ever dreamed."

She felt her desire for him stir. His hard body felt so good against hers that she wished she didn't have to let him go. But they both had to get back to work.

"I almost forgot. I brought something for you."

Her heart melted at his gesture. Even though they'd been dating for a few months, he never failed to bring her a little gesture of his affection whenever they spent time together.

He unwrapped a napkin and pulled out a daisy chain. He gave her a sheepish smile and threaded it into her hair.

"It's a little crushed, but all the petals are still there."

"You mean I can still play he loves me, he loves me not?"

His eyes darkened at her words. "You don't have to play games. You know how I feel about you. The problem is I don't know how you feel about me."

Her voice dropped to a whisper. "You said you would give me time."

He nodded, and she was relieved. "I know, and I'll still honor my word. But in the meantime, I want you to come to dinner tonight and meet my family."

Though she agreed without hesitation, internally she wasn't sure that meeting his parents and brother was a good idea.

Trent walked into the spacious kitchen juggling three apples in the air. His mother leaned her hip against the granite countertop and watched in mock amusement.

He caught all three safely and with a satisfied grin on his face, handed each one to her to wash.

"That was quite an entrance," she remarked. "I

haven't seen you do that in years. It couldn't be because I'm making my famous Waldorf salad."

He kissed her on the cheek. "I just wanted to entertain you."

"Bah!" Agnes laughed. She shooed him away with her hands. "It's that woman you're seeing. You must be pretty serious about her to invite her to dinner, not that I'm complaining. I've been waiting forever for you to find a wife."

He rolled his eyes. "Whoa! Hold on, Mom. I never said anything about marriage."

"Bah!" She handed him the washed apples. "It's time, Trent. You and your brother both need to settle down. Maybe then you'll stop being at each other's throats all the time."

He kept his eyes on the knife as he diced. "Steve is still sore at me about Violet. He lost her because he was more devoted to the almighty dollar than to her."

Agnes frowned. "He loves Waterson Builders, almost as much as his father, which might not be a good thing."

Trent handed her the bowl of apples. "What do you mean?"

"At first, the empty plate at the dinner table was your father, now it's you and your brother."

She waved a spoon in the air. "I guess we all work too much. We have to find a way back to what matters. A wedding is just the thing to give us all a kick in the pants to refocus on love and family."

"Don't go sending the invitations yet, Mom. I don't know how she feels about me."

She wrinkled her nose, as if offended. "Who wouldn't love any son of mine?"

Agnes retrieved two bottles of wine, red and white, from the pantry and set them on the counter.

"I don't know about Steve, but I'm the perfect catch for any woman," he joked.

There is only one woman for me.

He grabbed the corkscrew, and his hands shook a little as he opened the wine. He didn't tell his mother, but he was crazy nervous about the evening ahead. It had to go right. His family could be a little over-bearing for most people.

"Of course, you are," Agnes affirmed. "And if Sonya doesn't see it, then she's a fool. I sincerely can't wait to meet her."

She gave him a warm smile and a pat on the cheek. "No pressure."

"Thanks, Mom," he replied in a dry tone. "Just don't mention the *M* word, okay? I don't want her to run out on me."

"I promise." She winked. "And if I happen to slip up, I get the feeling you'll run right after her."

Trent smiled, and picked up three oranges from the basket on the counter to juggle his jitters away.

With much affection, he thought, *Why does my mother always have to be right?* He knew in his heart that he'd run after Sonya until he caught her, no matter how long it took.

Sonya eyed the expansive two-story colonial-style estate as she walked up to the door. It appeared to have more rooms than she would ever care to clean, and made her thankful for her home, which was more manageable.

Her home.

She always had to stop herself when she said or thought those words, because the house wasn't really hers. It belonged to her aunt, and technically the bank, which was worse because they had the power to take it away from both of them.

Sometimes she wished she were the type of person who could just live with a backpack and a tent as their sole possessions. But she loved taking hot showers, warm bubble baths and having a comfy bed to make love to Trent in.

She smoothed her hand over her pale blue linen suit. Even though she'd had the garment dry-cleaned, she'd forgotten how easily the fabric wrinkled, but wearing it made her feel more in control. On top of an empty belly full of nerves and the fact that she was ten minutes late for dinner, she wanted to turn around and get back in the car.

The door opened before she could even press the bell, and she felt herself being swooped off her feet.

Trent set her down and planted kisses all over her face.

Her heart fluttered in her chest from a combination of surprise and worry that his parents and brother were standing right behind him, like some sort of receiving line.

"Baby, I'm so glad you're all right! I tried texting you, but got no response."

She peered around his shoulder and breathed a huge sigh of relief that no one was there.

"I left my phone at home by mistake. And they were laying new tar on one side of the road I took to get here, so traffic got backed up. That's why I'm late. I'm sorry to keep everybody waiting."

He shut the door and ushered her inside. "No worries. They hopped on an emergency conference call, so they didn't notice."

He took her elbow and led her down the hall.

"I hope nothing is wrong," she said as he guided her into the brightly lit kitchen, one of the largest she'd ever seen.

"Nah, just another day in the cutthroat business of real estate." He held up two bottles of wine. "White or red?"

"Red, please."

She accepted a glass, which was followed by a

passionate kiss that sent tingles cascading through her body.

She stroked his chest, slightly embarrassed by his affection, but left her hand there, because she wasn't sure when she'd be able to touch him again that evening.

"Don't you think we should be on our best behavior tonight?"

His lips moved to her neck. "But it's so hard being good when we're together."

She felt his desire for her press against her body, and she had to stop herself from dropping her hand lower.

Sonya giggled as he began to nuzzle his nose behind her earlobe. "If you don't quit right now, I'm going to drop this wineglass on the floor."

He took a step back and sulked. "Okay, but only because my mother would kill me. Those are apparently very valuable, but don't ask me why."

They looked up when his mother walked into the room.

Sonya gulped when she made a beeline right for her.

"Why are you making me out to be such a fiend, Trent? Everything is replaceable.

"I'm Agnes Waterston, Sonya. Welcome to our home."

"Thank you," she replied, accepting the hug. "I'm happy to be here."

Agnes poured a glass of wine and looped her arm through Sonya's. "Come on into the dining room. My husband and Steve are still on a call, so we won't wait for them. We're doing buffet style tonight."

Trent grabbed the wine bottles, plus the rolls, which were warming up in the oven, and followed them.

"My mother made all the food. She's a great cook."

Agnes glanced behind her. "We used to have a personal chef, but I decided to start cooking again recently."

"She uses cooking as an excuse to get out of the office early," Trent said.

"That's right, and I'm not ashamed to admit it."

Agnes and Trent shared a knowing glance and began to laugh. Sonya was heartened by the easy repartee between mother and son, and some of the nervousness went away.

Trent lit the candles on the table, as Agnes pointed to the food on the sideboard. In addition to Waldorf salad, there were fried scallops, grilled shrimp on skewers, roasted potatoes and peppers. For dessert, Sonya spied a choice between apple and pecan pie.

Just as they were done filling their plates, Trent's father and brother spilled into the room. By their raised voices, it was apparent they were in the middle of a heated argument.

"I need you to fix this," Trent's father barked. "Like, yesterday!"

Steve patted him on the back. "I'm on it, Dad. Just as soon as Mom and I get back from Albuquerque."

"You see the trouble you got me in?"

Sonya thought Steve was talking to her, but he was speaking to Trent, who placed his hand on her shoulder.

"Boys, we have a guest. Please refrain from talking business at the dinner table."

"My mother is the peacemaker," Trent said before introducing his father and brother.

"And we make all the money." Steve winked, shaking her hand.

She sat down at the table, with Trent to her right. While everyone else was getting their food, he reached under the table and squeezed her hand.

"How's the new dance studio coming along?" Agnes asked as she sat down at the head.

Sonya slipped her hand away and picked up her fork.

"Nearly ready. I hope to open soon."

She'd hoped she wouldn't have to talk about her plans too much. She didn't feel like having to explain herself.

"Good. I plan on signing up for lessons myself," Agnes announced. She stared down the shocked looks of the men around the table. "What the devil are you all staring at me for? I heard ballet is very good exercise. After fifteen years of sitting at a desk, I need some toning."

"I'll be happy to have you as a student, Mrs. Waterston," Sonya replied, hiding a smile.

"You're not going to have time for much, Agnes, once we get the affordable housing project underway."

Sonya glanced at Trent. "That's wonderful. I've heard more housing is a real need in Bay Point."

"Yes, I'm looking for some land to build it on," Steve jumped in. "That's what my father and I were just talking about when we walked in."

Lawrence picked up a piece of shrimp. "The Maddox brothers turned us down. We're running out of options."

Trent sipped his wine. "Not a chance, Dad. Not with Steve on the loose."

Steve raised a brow and raised his glass. "You're sticking up for me? That deserves a toast."

"Only if you don't take what doesn't belong to you."

Sonya heard the undercurrent of a threat in Trent's tone. She felt Steve's eyes flicker toward her, and then they were back on his brother.

"Don't worry. I know my place."

Agnes and Lawrence seemed ignorant of whatever was transpiring between the two men. Even Sonya was confused, although she did remember

Trent saying at one time that he and Steve didn't really get along.

It was one more thing that they shared in common.

Neither had a perfect family.

Chapter 10

Trent secured the remaining stack of brochures with a rubber band and dropped them into a small box. Steve had texted him about two hours before the second annual Bay Point Home Expo had opened that he couldn't make it. So he'd called Sonya, who had agreed to help him at the booth.

He picked her up in his truck and drove to the high school, where the expo was being held in the gym and the first-floor hallways. He'd been able to sign up about ten people for appointments to view the remaining five lots in the company's latest development.

Though his brother and father wouldn't consider

the leads a true success until they had signed contracts and deposits in hand, his mother would be surprised at his efforts.

Ever since he was a little boy, Agnes had always encouraged him to work with his hands. She knew that a hammer in one hand and a couple of nails in the other was all that had ever made him happy. She didn't know that someone else had made all the houses he'd built over the years seem like he was playing with pixie sticks. He knew what happiness was now, being with Sonya and loving her, mind, body and soul.

She hadn't told him that she loved him, but in his heart, he knew that she did. He could tell by the way her breath caught every time he touched her hair. He loved to kiss her hand when he arrived on her doorstep, like an old Hollywood movie hero, because her lips would always tremble with surprise. And when he took her in his arms, she would cling to him, even if he'd only been away from her a short time.

Some force in the universe had thrown them together, and he would do all he could to keep them together forever.

Now, all Trent wanted to do was have a quick meal, a hot bath and climb into bed with Sonya.

"How can I ever thank you for helping me out today?"

Sonya finished wiping off the rental table and

tossed the paper towel in the trash can. "I'm sure I can think of a couple of ways," she said with a grin.

"With your active imagination, I can't wait to hear your ideas. What are you doing later?"

He waited in anticipation as she folded the red tablecloth and then put it on the chair.

"I'm sorry, Trent, but I'm busy tonight."

His heart clenched with disappointment. "Okay, I was hoping to spend some time alone with you."

Ever since the dinner at his parents' house earlier that week, Sonya had found excuses not to see him, and he was getting more than concerned. He was downright scared.

That evening, when she'd gotten home, he'd been overjoyed to receive a text from her soon after she arrived home. When he arrived, she was naked and she took him into her arms. Their lovemaking had been sweeter than ever, and he'd held her long into the night. He'd taken their time together as a celebration that they'd presented themselves as a couple to his family, and that she was ready to take the next step.

When he'd left the next morning, she'd been sleeping, so he hadn't been able to get her reaction to the dinner.

At that time, he'd assumed that she was okay with how the evening with his family had gone. But now, he wasn't so sure.

He grabbed a bunch of pens and shoved them in a plastic bag so hard that it broke.

She began to stack up the leftover magnets. "I didn't mean to upset you, Trent."

"You didn't," he lied and threw the bag away. "You don't have to explain anything to me."

She lowered her voice, mindful of the people still milling around the room.

"I know, but sometimes I feel like I should."

He stowed the pens in another box. "It's been a long day for both of us. Why don't I just take you home?"

She waited as he did a last spot check of the space to make sure everything was cleared out before they made their way outside to his truck.

When they got there, Trent opened the passenger side for Sonya, and then stuffed the box in the back seat.

He got in, put on his seat belt and backed out. He thought about taking the long way, just to have more time with her, but she seemed distracted. It was killing him not to know what it was, like having a mosquito bite in a place he couldn't reach.

"Why don't you tell me what's wrong?" he asked.

She glanced over at him. "I thought you said I didn't have to explain."

"You don't, but I wish you would. I care about you so much."

He drummed his fingers on the steering wheel as they waited for a red light to flip over to green.

She stared out the passenger window. "How can I when I don't know myself?"

"Maybe I can help."

She bit her lip and turned toward him in her seat. "There is something that has been bothering me. While you and Steve were clearing the dishes, and your mom was making coffee, your father asked me a strange question."

"What did he ask?"

"He'd heard about my father's gambling debts, which isn't surprising, because practically everyone in town knows my dad had a problem. They laughed at him behind his back.

"No one says it to my face," she continued. "But I still think some people blame me for my father's downfall, and maybe they're right. Maybe it is my fault he gambled his life away."

Trent heard the shame in her voice, and it splintered his heart. "We've talked about this before, Sonya, and we both know it's not your fault."

She wrung her hands in her lap. "How can you be so sure? My aunt said he got worse after I left Bay Point. At first, it was poker games with his friends once or twice a week, and then the trips to Vegas. It was like he had nothing left to lose."

"We can't be responsible for the actions or motivations of our parents."

She furrowed her brow. "Like the fact that your father insinuated that I was going out with you for your money. You know I don't care anything about your wealth. I told him the same thing, but I'm not sure if he believed me."

He felt his stomach clench at her words. It was bad enough having his mom ask him when he was going to get married, but to have his dad butt into his love life and practically accuse Sonya of being a gold digger was just too much.

"Don't take it personal. My dad was just having a knee-jerk reaction to the type of women Steve normally brings around. Why, Violet was the only woman he's ever dated that was worth marrying."

"I think Violet still cares about him," Sonya mused. "She only went after you to make him jealous."

"If Steve would ever wise up, he'd know it, too. My father razzed me for years because I broke up with my college girlfriend."

"Was she cute?" Sonya interjected with a hint of a smile.

He shrugged. "She was okay in a college coed kind of way. She wanted me to be more about business than construction. To her, working with my hands was a little too blue-collar for her, and my father has a similar attitude. It never would have worked."

Although she looked unconvinced, he knew she had nothing to worry about. Given time, his father would come around and see Sonya as a wonderful choice for a wife. His mother was already smitten, and Trent expected her nudges to marry would increase.

"It doesn't matter what my father believes, or anyone else. All that matters is you and me and what we think about each other."

He felt her eyes on his face, and he wished they were sitting across from each other while having this conversation. It would have made it a lot easier.

"I just don't want to be the cause of any tension in your family. I've already broken up mine. I don't want the same to happen to yours."

He placed his hand on her thigh. "You don't have to worry. While we have our disagreements, the Watersons always prevail. We wouldn't have amassed the amount of land and property we have without working together as a family."

She turned her head toward him. "It's just me and Aunt Nelda now. We have to stick together, too."

"Any news on what she plans to do with the house?"

"No, nothing. Whenever I ask her, she changes the subject."

"Why do you think your aunt is keeping you in the dark? Do you think she's doing it on purpose?"

"Like your brother not showing up for duty?"

"There's no subterfuge with Steve. If he doesn't feel like doing something, he simply doesn't do it. Period."

"Anyway, I keep worrying that I'll come home one day to an eviction notice."

"That's not going to happen, Sonya."

"It could, and frankly, I'm scared."

He heard the catch in her voice and wished he could pull her into his arms. Instead, he took her hand in his and squeezed gently.

"If it does, you have a safe place to go. You'll stay with me."

She slipped her hand away. "You can't spend your life rescuing me, Trent."

"Why not?" he asked. "I love you."

She closed her eyes. "Don't say that, Trent."

"It's true," he sputtered. "And if I weren't driving and if I wouldn't get a ticket for indecent exposure, I'd show you just how much."

Her laugh bubbled up and gave him hope. "I don't doubt it."

"Then let me show you—when we get to your house, of course," he said, taking her hand in his again. "I think I can wait that long. Can you?"

"No," she whispered. "No, I really can't."

She rested her left hand between her thighs and he groaned. Not because that was all she did. But because that was enough, and he knew what her actions meant.

She kept her gaze on the road, as did he, although he knew his need for her could be felt, and his excitement barely contained. And for once, he was glad he'd taken the shortcut home, because every few minutes she would hike up her navy blue skirt a few millimeters with her right hand, exposing her thigh to him more and more.

Out of the corner of his eye, he saw the delicate lace of her bra, curved against her breast as she undid a few buttons of her shirt. His mouth watered a little more with every pop of her button.

And yet, her hand didn't move, even as he grew harder and harder, hot as a volcano.

By the time they were on the road that led to her house, he was so turned on that he almost missed her driveway.

When they were safely stopped and under the cover of her garage, she had her seat belt off before he did.

She hurriedly unzipped his pants and leaned over. He put his hand on her arm to stop her.

"I know I must be crazy to refuse you, but you've got me too hot. You'll make me explode with that sweet mouth of yours."

He pushed his seat back as far as it would go, and quickly lifted his polo shirt up and over his head.

"Climb over here, baby."

She kissed up his bare forearm and licked the bend of his elbow. All he could think about was that he wished her tongue could be in two places on his body at one time.

"Hurry up, Sonya. You're driving your man crazy."

Her sultry smile let him know that she was going to take her time getting to him, and there was nothing he could do about it.

He grunted when she arrived, settling her lower half on his thighs as if they'd belonged there forever. She gyrated against him slowly as he devoured her mouth in a passionate kiss.

"Am I your woman, Trent? You're only one?"

"You know you are." He bunched her hair in his hand and nuzzled her neck. "I love you, Sonya. And if it takes a million years for you to admit that you love me, too, I'll wait."

She hiked up her skirt around her trim waist. "I promise you won't have to wait for me that long. You can have me right now."

He gazed up into her eyes. "You aren't a high school crush or a weekend fling. I love you! I want your heart and your body. Don't you realize that?"

She leaned her back against the steering wheel. He stared at her delicate black panties that he'd bought for her.

He pressed his thumb against the wettest spot, and she threw her head back, her curls cascading over her shoulders.

Her moan drew out and reverberated throughout the space, and ended in a sharp intake of breath.

"Trent, do that again, please!"

He pressed again, and rotated his thumb in a tiny circle against the fabric. His eyes glazed over with the need to see, and feel and taste all the passion she had for him.

He made a split-second decision. The panties were expensive, but they had to go. He ripped them in half and tossed the damp pieces of lace in the back seat.

"I'll buy you some new ones, even prettier than these."

Now she was completely, beautifully exposed to him.

"Oh, Trent, what are we doing?" she breathed, looking down at him.

"What we do best, baby," he muttered thickly, planting a kiss on her slit of a navel. "Pleasing one another."

Loving one another.

They both knew there wasn't much room in his truck, but they were determined to make it work. He reclined the seat back as far as it would go. She squatted over him while he cupped her buttocks to support her weight.

She shrugged out of her shirt. Now, all she had on was her bra made of sheer black lace, and he would get rid of that soon.

He wished he could take off her pencil skirt, but he would never get it past her melon-shaped breasts. He left it alone, bunched up around her waist.

She whimpered in anticipation as he squeezed her buttocks to edge her closer to him.

"You know what I was thinking of the entire time you were next to me today?"

He ducked and nudged her thighs apart with his head.

As she planted her heels on the seat, he inhaled her sweet womanly scent and his mouth began to water.

"Never mind, I'll just show you."

He darted his tongue deep inside her quickly and then up and around her folds, sucking gently. He thought he knew exactly what to do to make her body pulse against him. Yet, each time he placed his mouth against her most intimate areas, he discovered more ways to please her. He loved the way she seemed to cave into his mouth, and to the will of his tongue.

His penis throbbed almost painfully as he repeated his movements over and over. And sometimes, he had to pause and take a breath, and her hands clawed at his hair, urging him to continue.

She breathed quickly, almost hyperventilating, with the pleasure he was giving her. When her legs started to quiver, he knew it was time. He withdrew his tongue and she collapsed on top of him, and he hurried to shed his pants.

The lack of room in the truck made their movements somewhat cautious, but somehow he was able to roll her with him until she was on her back. She reached her hands up and held on to the headrest, while he unhooked her bra. Her breasts bounced as they moved together, nipples stiff and enticing. He forced himself to look away. He knew if he kissed her there, he was a goner.

Their bodies were slick with sweat as he held her tight to him. Her legs shot up and her feet flattened against the ceiling as he rocked inside her, crooning her name in her ear.

He withdrew and thrust himself into her, and her hips rose again and again to meet him. They bucked together violently, caught in a cage of their own desire. She came without warning, biting his shoulder, so she wouldn't cry out. She dug her fingers into the small of his back, something she'd never done before, and he felt the life spurt out of him and into her.

They lay there for a while, as he kissed her and played with her nipples, until she was writhing beneath him again. He loved her so much that he could pleasure her all night long, while taking nothing more for himself.

The windows were steamed up, and he opened the car door to get some air. They shifted positions and she climbed back into the passenger seat to fix her clothes.

"Can we continue this inside?" he asked, knowing it wouldn't be long before he was ready to make love to her again. His need for her was insatiable.

She leaned over and gave him a kiss. "I want to be alone tonight, Trent."

He pulled on his pants and zipped them up. He couldn't help but feel hurt and rejected. "So I guess you do still think we're seeing too much of one another."

"I'm not going to answer that question right now."

She finished buttoning up her shirt and looked back toward the house. He wondered if someone were waiting for her there, but there were no other cars in her driveway.

She said goodbye and got out, and he watched her hips sway seductively in the rearview mirror as she walked away.

"I'm going to keep asking until you answer, until you realize that I'm here for you, Sonya, and I'm not going away."

When she was safely inside, he backed out of the driveway and headed home.

Sonya picked up the final twig from the front lawn, then shaded her eyes and looked up at the house. Now that there was a strong possibility of losing it, she was beginning to cherish it all the more.

In the past several months, she'd managed to complete several repairs. She installed a ceiling fan in her bedroom, which got a workout cooling her and Trent after their extended lovemaking sessions. With his help, she'd even installed a new mantel over the living room fireplace.

She wiped her brow. It was not yet noon, and the temperature was already in the mideighties. She got a bottle of water out of the cooler on the porch and sat on the step.

Lately, she'd gotten in the habit of sitting outside whenever she could, just to think. The view wasn't nearly as pretty as it was out back, but she still loved to count the cars that drove by. There weren't many. The area where she lived wasn't heavily populated and was dotted with farms and ranches. She wondered how long they would last.

Often, her thoughts turned to Trent, and she wondered what it would be like to spend the rest of her days and nights with him. To be the mother of his children.

She knew that she couldn't keep putting off discussing their relationship. It wasn't fair to him or to both of them to be in such a state of limbo, but that was exactly where she was in her life right now. And he just happened to be along for the ride.

A car crunched up the long gravel driveway. The twang of a blues guitar streamed out of the open window as Nelda pulled up to the house. Her aunt was smiling for the first time in months, and that alone made Sonya's insides ring with hope.

"Yoo-hoo, Sonya!" Nelda called out as she got out of the car.

"I could have called you on the phone, but I wanted to tell you in person."

She set down her water bottle and rose to meet her. "What's going on, Auntie?"

"You won't believe what's happened," she rasped, as if out of breath. "I've got some wonderful news. All of our troubles are over. In no time at all, I'm going to have the money to pay off the mortgage."

"That's wonderful. Where did you get it? Did you win the lottery?"

Nelda shook her finger. "Hush, Sonya. You know I don't gamble. This is better than the lottery. The Watersons are buying it."

She inhaled sharply. "You mean Trent?" She'd started to say *my boyfriend*, but stopped herself just in time. She didn't know how much Nelda knew about their relationship, if anything at all.

Nelda shook her head. "No, his brother, Steve, called me originally, but he told me that Trent said that you told him I was interested in selling."

"I never told Trent any such thing. I thought you and I agreed we wouldn't sell it."

"We both knew I didn't have the money to pay the back mortgage. We also knew that the bank held all the power in this scenario."

"I know," Sonya admitted. "But I'd hoped that somehow we could find a way."

"You've always been such a dreamer." Her aunt put her hands on her hips. "Did you expect us to find a pot of gold at the end of a rainbow? That's a risk I didn't want to take. A foreclosure would have ruined my credit for the rest of my life. Besides, what are you and I going to do with eight-hundred acres of land?"

"Well, we could start our own winery. I had the soil tested, and it's suitable for a number of grape varieties."

"A winery? At my age?" Nelda choked out. "I'm retired. Besides, what about your dance studio?"

"I could do both," Sonya insisted, even though deep down, she knew she was being overzealous. "Okay, I couldn't, at least not right now. I was just trying to be creative."

Her aunt folded her arms at her chest. "But there's no need, Sonya. I'm selling the house and the land to the Waterson brothers. They're giving us about twenty percent over the appraised value of the land. After the mortgage is paid off, there's enough left over for each of us to do what we want."

She bit her lip. "What will happen to the home?"

Nelda paused, and then frowned. "It'll be razed, of course. That's the first thing that will be done, but don't worry. Steve said Trent would handle that part of it."

Sonya felt like she was going to faint at the thought of Trent at the helm of the bulldozer that in a matter of minutes would destroy all the wonderful memories they'd created in nearly every room in the house.

"That will never happen," she vowed. "Never!"

Nelda gave her an odd look. "Of course it will. Our home will be replaced with what Steve called 'affordable bungalows.' Isn't that wonderful?"

"Yes, wonderful," she replied glumly.

"I tried to get Steve to call the development Young Condominiums, as a tribute to us, but he wasn't too keen on the idea. He told me his mother usually names them."

She folded her hands in her lap. "I guess it's all settled."

Her aunt nodded. "I'm afraid so, Sonya. I know you've come to love this house. Although it wasn't that long ago that you couldn't wait to leave it."

"I know. I was just hoping…" Her voice trailed off.

To make a life with Trent in it.

"This will give us both enough money. If it weren't for my investments, I don't know what I'd do. I won't have to worry now. And neither will you."

"I know, Auntie. I had such plans for this home. I was willing to take a loan against the studio, but the repayment terms would have been every thirty days. The risk was too high."

"You made the right decision. You can still make plans, but with some other home, and some other place. Maybe Trent's?"

Sonya held back a gasp. "What do you mean?"

Nelda smiled. "I don't pry into your business, but I know you two have been dating."

"Oh, you're not prying. I've just been quiet about it, because I wasn't sure if it was going to last."

"And do you think it will?"

Sonya shrugged. "Maybe."

"I'm surprised Trent didn't tell you about this. His brother said he'd mentioned it at your dinner."

She didn't want to tell Nelda that Steve was a liar. And maybe his brother was, too.

When Sonya didn't answer, Nelda put her hands over her lips. "Oh, I hope I didn't ruin things between you two."

"I'll be okay." She hugged her aunt and forced a smile. "We both will."

"Thank you for understanding, dear. You don't know how happy that makes me. I was so worried that you'd hate me.

"Hate you? After all you've done for me and my father? That just isn't possible."

Sonya knew that as bookkeeper, Nelda had managed the store's finances as best as she could. But her father, who'd managed the inventory, often sold jewels or pawned them in other cities without her knowing. He would disappear to Las Vegas for days and come back hungover and flat broke. It was a wonder Nelda hadn't lost the house sooner.

She walked with her aunt back to the car. She opened the door for her. "So what happens next?"

"I'm having my lawyer review the contract, and I'll call you when everything is signed, so you'll have plenty of notice to find a new place to live."

Nelda got in and stuck her hand out of the open window. "Are you sure you're okay with this?"

She held back her tears and forced another smile.

"Who knows, maybe when the homes are built, I'll buy one. Then it will be like I never even left."

"That's the spirit, Sonya!"

Sonya waved goodbye and backtracked until she hit the porch steps. She sank down and buried her head in her hands. A whirlwind of emotions went through her body. She sat there a long time, until she figured out what she had to do next, and she realized she'd never had any real choice at all.

Chapter 11

Sonya disembarked from Trent's motorcycle with a silent prayer that they'd both arrived at her home in one piece. Trent had already proven to be an excellent driver, and he was extra careful when she was riding with him. It was the other people on the road that worried her.

During their time together over the past week, she'd tried to work up the courage to mention the pending sale of her aunt's home. She kept hoping he would bring it up first, but he never did. She was tired of the games.

She gave him a weary smile. "I can't believe you got me on this thing again."

"Second time's a charm." He winked.

She tucked the snazzy red-and-black helmet he'd bought for her under her arm. She felt sad that this was probably the last time she would be able to feel the freedom of the open road unwinding before them.

"I do believe that bike is growing on me, and so are you."

Her words were from the heart, and if she hadn't felt betrayed, she would have told him that she loved him.

But it was too late.

Trent stowed their helmets. "I've been waiting months to hear you say that!"

He snagged the belt loop of her jeans with the crook of his finger and pulled her to him. "C'mere."

He planted a kiss near her ear, and she giggled out a warning. "Don't get too excited. I still prefer to travel by car."

The cuffs of his leather jacket grazed her jaw as he pulled her into a long, sweet kiss. When it ended, she didn't want to open her eyes. She wished she could stay in the bubble of his affection forever.

"I'd chauffeur you anywhere, by camel, by elephant, by any means necessary, just as long as we're together."

She heard the commitment in his voice and her eyes started to burn with tears. If he'd only told her of his family's plans, everything would have been different.

He lifted her chin with the pad of his thumb. "Open your eyes, Sonya."

When she was sure she wouldn't cry, she did. "You're very sweet, you know that?"

He gave her another kiss. "You make it easy to be that way. I really appreciate you coming out to my place today. I've been wanting to show it to you for a while."

She clicked her tongue behind her teeth. "It's your fault, Trent. You've kept us so busy at mine that we just haven't had the time."

"I take full responsibility." Trent molded her curves with his hands and pressed his body to hers. "We ran out of rooms to make love in at your house a long time ago."

"The attic doesn't count, remember?" she murmured, as he threaded his fingers through her hair.

"Don't worry, baby. There are plenty of rooms to explore at my place, and we have all the time in the world."

His lips moved over hers, and their tongues met. She began to melt into his kiss, but managed to step away just as he tried to deepen it.

Her eyes traveled south and spotted the enormous bulge in his pants. The fact that she was able to elicit such an intense physical reaction from simply kissing him made her want to forget the pain he and his family had caused her.

Still, she wanted to do nothing more at that moment than touch him.

When they got inside, Trent took her hand in his and kissed it.

"Did you like it?" he asked. "I know it's just a model home, but everything is brand-new."

She ran the fingers of her other hand through her hair to quell her desire. "Well, it certainly is big."

Her veiled compliment to him was lost on him as he proudly extolled its virtues.

"Five bedrooms and three baths," Trent continued. "A huge pool in the backyard. There's enough garage space to squeeze in an extra car, and a motorcycle for you, if you'd ever let me buy one for you."

Her mind went back to his contemporary mansion. There were no curves to the walls, no arches on the windows and worse, no history. It was all right angles and straight lines, more glamorous than his parents' home, and ultimately, not her style.

"It's beautiful and I enjoyed seeing it, but to tell you the truth, I'd never be comfortable in such a sizeable home."

He frowned. "I'd hoped that someday you would want to live there with me."

She sat down on the sofa. "I'm sorry, Trent. It just wouldn't work. I'm too used to this place. It's old and needs work, but it's comfortable. I want to enjoy it as long as I can."

He eased in next to her. "I understand your attachment to this home. I just hoped we could spend some more time at mine. I know you would come to love it as much as I do. No work, more play."

"Has it ever crossed your mind that there's something wrong with taking land that was previously populated only by trees and animals and putting up ginormous homes that only a few can afford?"

He furrowed his brow. "Most of our customers are busy people who want move-in ready homes with top-of-the-line appliances and luxury interiors. Everything is brand-new. When they come home, they can just enjoy it, not tackle the next project on their list."

Sonya folded her arms. "I haven't done so bad with this place, have I?"

"You've done a fantastic job, and I'm proud of you. Most people would have just given up and bought new," he responded. "Honestly, I thought you would have put a hold on your to-do list for the house, until you heard more about what was going to happen with it."

"I feel it's important to live my life as if it's not about to fall apart at any second."

He put his arm around her shoulders. "That's why I'm offering you my home, because I don't want you to worry. I want you to enjoy life."

She slid away and turned to him. "I won't live in your home."

"Don't you think you should have a fallback plan?

If you move in with me, you can open your studio and concentrate on teaching dance. Isn't that what you want?"

She felt her heart tug at the concern in his voice, and she almost wished that her aunt had chosen to save the home instead of the jewelry store.

"I'm not sure what I want anymore. All I know is that I want to stay here. This is my home. Things between us are happening so fast. Now you want me to move in with you."

"I'm not saying you need to move in right now. I just wanted to help."

Sonya stood and walked over to the mantel. "I appreciate the offer. I feel like I don't even have time to think anymore. There's too much pressure on me."

He went to her and placed his hands on her shoulders, and she rested her forehead against the mantel.

"I can give you all the time you need."

She rubbed her thumb along the polished wood. "I think it's best that we take a break."

"So I've finally got my answer." He blew out a long breath. "For how long?"

"I don't know, Trent. Everything is up in the air. Where I'm going to live, when I'm going to open the studio. I'm not even sure I want to stay in Bay Point."

He turned her around to face him. "Why? What's really going on here?"

She debated confiding what she knew and asking him to help her. But what good would that do? She didn't want to put him in the position of choosing his family's business over his love for her. Her father had asked her to make a choice, and she'd ended up estranged from him.

It was her hope that if she and Trent could no longer be lovers, at least they could be friends.

"I can't discuss it. All I will say is that your family is involved. Why don't you ask them?"

Trent swallowed hard. "I don't understand. I know that my father got the wrong impression of you and our relationship, but I haven't had a chance to set him straight."

Although she should have been happy, Sonya felt a flash of disappointment that he didn't seem to know more. He'd always told her he didn't get involved in business matters, but she'd found that hard to believe. Maybe he'd been telling the truth.

"We had dinner with them over a week ago and you haven't had a conversation with your father yet? I guess it just wasn't that important to you."

"I was planning on talking to him after the staff meeting tomorrow, but now I'm wondering if it really matters."

"Has your patience run out?"

"Not yet, but I can't guarantee that it won't."

Perhaps her father had been right all along. Maybe she really did deserve to live her life alone.

"I'm sorry, Trent. I don't know when I can see you again."

She was losing her home to the Watersons. The only thing she didn't know was why Trent wouldn't admit it.

"I guess that's it." He dropped his hands to his sides and strode to the door. She thought he was going to walk out without saying anything, but he just stood there with his hand on the doorknob.

"Just call me when you figure things out or don't. It's really up to you."

When he left, she closed her eyes. Her indecision had caused her to break Dewayne's heart, and now Trent's.

The sun streamed through the conference room windows, but Trent didn't bother adjusting the blinds. He hoped the bright light would wake him up, because the coffee sure wasn't.

He'd been up before dawn. After spending the night tossing and turning, he'd decided to head to the office early. The receptionist wasn't even there yet to unlock the main door. He used his own key for the first time in years.

Ten minutes later, he'd figured out how to use the industrial coffeemaker, a task that should have taken ten seconds.

Time was going in slow motion, ever since yesterday. His body couldn't keep up, yet his heart was shattered. It still hadn't sunk in that Sonya had broken up with him.

The excitement of showing his home had quickly dissipated when she told him she wouldn't live with him.

It had been so unexpected that he hadn't wanted to believe it. And every time he thought about believing it was over, his stomach hurt so bad that he'd thought about calling a doctor.

We can't be over. We're so good together.

He grabbed the carafe and poured himself another cup of coffee. He put it to his lips but didn't drink. What had he done to make her turn against him?

"Besides inviting her to dinner with my parents," he muttered. He set the cup down with a clatter. That had been a mistake, at least where his father was concerned.

He racked his brain, trying to think of what he could have done differently in the relationship. Perhaps he'd been too overbearing with all the gifts, but they'd been from his heart. Maybe he was too affectionate, but she was beautiful and the longer he was with her, the more he wanted her. They'd been dating over six months and though they were more comfortable with one another, there'd been no warning sign that she was bored or dissatisfied with the relationship.

An hour later, his thoughts were interrupted by the voices of his mother, brother and father in the reception area, which was just outside the conference room. The excitement in their voices roused him from his chair.

He went out to greet them. "Nice of you all to show up to work today."

"Hi, Trent," his mother exclaimed. "What are you doing here so early?"

"Yeah, what's the special occasion?" his brother piped in.

"Where's Judy?" Lawrence bellowed, ignoring them all.

He took off his pork pie hat and stowed it in the closet. "She's supposed to be here by now."

"She has the day off," Agnes soothed. "You'll have to answer your own phones today."

"You're lucky I'm in a good mood," his father barked.

"Just do like I do, Dad. Let them all go to voice mail," Steve advised.

He put his arm around Trent's neck and squeezed it playfully. "You will be happy to learn that one of your expo leads came through. Signed the contract yesterday. Now you just have to reel in the other four."

"I told you we picked up some good leads, but you didn't believe me," Trent said.

"We?" Lawrence enquired.

Steve sat on the edge of the receptionist's desk. "His girlfriend, Sonya, helped him at the booth."

"Because he was a no-show," Trent said, pointing

at his brother, who rolled his eyes. "It was a good thing she was there. The auditorium was packed and we had a lot of interest."

Agnes glanced over at her husband with a triumphant smile. "Didn't I tell you she was the perfect woman for Trent? She's already interested in the family business."

"Don't tell him that, Mom. He's already accused Sonya of being a gold digger."

Agnes turned on her husband, who immediately looked away. "You did what?"

"After the dinner, he accused Sonya of dating me just for my money."

His mother gave him a quick hug. "I'm so sorry. Did you tell her that your father is all bluster and no bones?"

Trent ignored his dad's exaggerated scowl. "I tried, but she wouldn't listen. She has a lot on her mind."

"Focus on the business, Trent, and you'll never have to worry about a broken heart," Steve advised. "Hopefully, those other leads will come through soon."

"Thanks for the advice. You're a real romantic," Trent said in a wry tone.

He leaned back in his chair. "It's too bad we don't have a location for the affordable housing project yet. That would have been a great event to promote it, but there's always next year."

Lawrence cleared his throat. "Let's go into the conference room. I want to make you aware of some recent developments with that project."

When they were all settled, Steve clapped his hands together. "Dad, let me explain it to him. We just came from a breakfast meeting with a landowner—Nelda Young."

"Sonya's aunt." Trent felt his stomach drop, and he slammed a fist down on the table. "Didn't I tell you weeks ago not to approach her?"

"Let your brother finish," Lawrence admonished.

"Poor woman," Steve continued, "I know you told me not to talk to her, but she was in such dire straits that I couldn't resist. I saw her at Carousel Park and told her that Sonya had told you that she was interested in selling. And Nelda did not disagree. She wanted to do a deal, so that's what we did."

"We got her out of a bind, and she did the same for us."

"How much did we pay her?"

Steve squeezed his fingers together. "A pinch over and above the appraised cost of the land. Enough to pay off the mortgage and give Nelda a nice nest egg for her remaining years."

"That's touching, Steve. And what about the house?"

His brother clapped his hands. "That's the bonus. You get to do what you do best. Raze it!"

Trent closed his eyes briefly. It pained him to

think that he would have to bulldoze Sonya's childhood home to the ground.

"Nelda ran into financial trouble bailing her brother out of his debts, and ended up not being able to pay her mortgage. I'm surprised Sonya didn't tell you."

Trent folded his arms and his expression turned grim. "Sonya did tell me. She also said she didn't want her aunt to sell the house. I can't believe you went behind both of our backs."

He realized with a sinking feeling that Nelda must have told Sonya about the deal. It was the only explanation for why she wanted a break in the relationship.

"It wasn't either of your decision to make," Steve said.

"True, but you didn't have to help it along for our gain." Trent scowled.

His brother didn't have a clue, nor did anyone in his family, how badly their actions had hurt his relationship with Sonya.

"Not just our gain, but the entire Bay Point community," Lawrence enthused. "I can't wait until we announce it. I'll bet we'll be sold out before we even break ground!"

Not if I can help it.

"Can I see the contracts, Mom?"

"Sure, honey. I've got it right here to scan into the system. Signed and countersigned." Agnes reached into her bag and gave him a thick document.

Trent took it from her and pretended to read. The price Steve had negotiated with Nelda was more than fair. There weren't many people who made money out of an all-out mortgage buy-out, but Nelda would. Plus, by avoiding foreclosure, she would protect her credit score.

"Wait until you see our profit margin on this deal," Steve said, and the excitement in his voice bubbled into a huge smile.

"I have no doubt that Waterson Builders will make a lot of money, even if the homes are supposed to be affordable," Trent affirmed, holding back a smirk.

"It's a good thing you're here," Agnes remarked. "I was going to ask you to drop this off at Nelda's apartment so we can save on postage. She said she didn't want the contract emailed."

Trent stood up, document in hand. "I don't think that will be necessary, Mother."

Before anyone could stop him, he savagely ripped the contract into pieces, starting with the signature page. With every tear, hope that he could mend things with Sonya became stronger in his heart.

Amid the shrieks from his mother, the curses from his father and the murderous stares from Steve, he continued shredding the document until there was just a pile of large white flecks on the conference room table.

He tossed the papers hither and yon around the

table, and they floated down like confetti in a ticker-tape parade.

"This is what happens when you try to screw around with the family of the woman I love."

"Do you realize what you just did?" Steve thundered.

Lawrence shook his head. "I told you he wouldn't like it."

Agnes clasped her hands to her chest. "Did you say love?"

Trent ignored them all and put his palms flat on the table. "Starting right now, I'm officially taking over this affordable housing project, including the land acquisition. When we meet next week, I will provide an update."

His father folded his arms across his chest and didn't say anything for a moment.

"That's fine, Trent. I've been waiting for a long time for you to help out in other areas of the business. This is the perfect chance for you to prove yourself."

Trent shook his head. "You don't get it, Dad. This is a one-and-done. Once I fix this, I'm back to doing what I love to do. Building and construction."

"Doesn't anybody care about the money we're about to lose?" Steve complained.

"Money isn't what's kept your father and I married all these years," Agnes said. "When a man is in love, he will do anything to keep his woman, and keep her happy."

"Your mother is right," Lawrence grumbled. "Do what you need to do. We trust that it'll be right for you and your family."

Trent got a large envelope out of the credenza and scooped all of the torn papers into it, just in case Steve got the idea to try to tape all the pieces together. He smiled, tucked the envelope under his arm and walked out of the room.

Chapter 12

The curtains puffed into the open window as Sonya wrapped some treasured family photos in craft paper. Though her aunt had given her plenty of notice to pack up, the task was still difficult and time-consuming. She'd been preparing for this day mentally for several weeks and had a new place to live.

Her apartment above the antique store was small, but it was within walking distance to the dance studio. The lease was month to month, so there was no long-term commitment. It would give her the time to think about what to do next.

With the family home sold and her relationship

with Trent now ended, she was trying to find a reason to stay in Bay Point.

Tears rolled down Sonya's face as she taped up her last box. She'd already packed up her father's clothes to donate to charity. In an old coat, she'd found a letter of apology, written to her shortly before he died, where he stated how sorry he was that he hadn't supported her dreams and that he wasn't more involved in her life.

She knew she would treasure her father's letter more than anything else she owned. She didn't have much more than clothes and personal mementos, having sold most of her furnishings when she'd left San Francisco.

Her insides hurt whenever she thought about Trent. Though he probably didn't realize it now, Sonya felt that breaking up had to be good for both of them. It was for the best. He was so connected to Bay Point, and she simply wasn't anymore.

Sonya wandered outside and sat down on the swing. She planted her bare heels into the grass and began to rock back and forth. When the swing began to sway, her mood lightened a bit. She thought about her father's letter, which had ended with him encouraging her to stay strong and follow her heart.

As she swung, she imagined her father doing the same thing. Casting his cares away by the swing of his feet. Forgetting about his troubles, his debts, his late wife, her.

If it were only that simple, she thought, remembering how she'd tried to forget her pain through endless hours of practice. Long after it was time to go home.

Until her feet bled through her shoes.

The sun had lowered, setting the sky ablaze in pinks and oranges. In the distance, the waves washed over the rocky shore in a violent kiss on endless repeat. If she listened hard enough, she could hear the ocean, just as she could hear her heart beating whenever Trent held her in his arms.

Her chin quivered as tears threatened to spill down her cheeks again. This was the last night she would spend in the home where she'd spent her formidable years.

Confused, alone.

It was only her dreams that kept her alive at that time. Eventually, they came true—but not without sacrifice. At least she'd held on to herself and her belief that one day she'd feel whole again.

A short time later, she was woken up from a short nap by a honk of a car.

She yawned, stretched and walked down the steps to greet Nelda, who was already out of her vehicle. The two women hugged.

"I just wanted to stop by and see if you were okay."

Sonya nodded. "I will spend one last night here and the movers will be here tomorrow morning."

The fact was that Nelda was her last remaining

relative. Her mother had no sisters and her maternal grandparents had already passed away before she was born.

"I'm sad, but I'll live. I think I've made my peace with the memories of this house."

"What about your father?"

Sonya let out a sigh. "I'm working on it. I used to think that living here again would help me deal with the loss. I never really knew my dad, Nelda, and that makes me saddest of all. I found a letter of apology in one of his pockets, and that eased my mind, but I wish he would have had the courage to send it to me while he was alive."

Nelda gave a grim nod. "Your father was a complicated man. I think he felt a lot of guilt for convincing your mother to move to the west coast."

"She was a grown woman. She made a choice to follow her heart and move."

"She was in love."

"He didn't have the store then, so he wasn't rich. I wonder what made her move so far away from everything she wanted?"

"Bay Point, at one time, back in the golden age of cinema, was known as a getaway for the Hollywood elite. Perhaps that was the draw. She was chasing another dream. Or maybe she just wanted to take a risk and have an adventure."

"Sound familiar?" Nelda asked.

Sonya smiled, and felt a new kinship with her

mother and her father. He was just an ordinary man who'd fallen in love with a beautiful dancer.

"I do hope this didn't spoil things between you and your boyfriend."

"Former boyfriend."

Nelda frowned. "Oh, no. I'm so sorry."

Sonya felt the sting of tears in her eyes, but she held them back. "Have you ever been in love, Nelda?"

She heard a deep sigh rattle in Nelda's chest, and moments passed before her aunt spoke.

"Once. He was a traveling salesman who specialized in designer watches. He used to come into the store and try to sell me the latest tickers, but we never bought any. Anyway, one day he asked me to walk on the beach with him. He gave me one of the watches as a present. And I realized, under the moonlight, that I loved him."

Sonya closed her eyes briefly and imagined the scene. When she opened them, her aunt was gazing at the sky. "Did you tell him how you felt?"

Nelda leveled her head and sighed. "No, I never did. I guess it was a combination of my being afraid and thinking there would always be time to do so."

The two women were silent as Sonya walked with Nelda to her car.

"Whatever happened to him and the watch?" Sonya asked in a quiet tone.

"Your father was a stickler for quality. He wanted only the best. When he learned from another jeweler that the watches the man was selling were not designer at all, but cheap knock-offs, I never saw the man again."

She gave Nelda a tight hug. "I'm sorry, Auntie."

Sonya waved goodbye as Nelda backed out the driveway, and wondered if anyone in her family would ever have a happy ending.

Trent checked his reflection in the rearview mirror. He was exhausted, but thankfully didn't look it. In the last week, he'd hustled like he'd never done before, but everything was set. He just hoped that Sonya would agree to the terms.

He ambled up the driveway slowly, flinching with every pop of the gravel under his tires. As he came around the bend, he was relieved to see that Sonya was not on the porch. Hopefully, she wasn't looking out the window.

This was an unannounced visit, and everything had to go perfectly.

He got out of the car and decided to check the backyard first. As planned, Nelda had visited Sonya a few minutes earlier, so she was definitely home.

He tiptoed around the side of the house and peeked around the corner.

Sonya was sitting on the swing, rocking in the breeze, her curls billowing out over her shoulders.

He swallowed hard, gathering courage, and when

he was as close as he dared, he deliberately stepped on the sycamore twigs scattered about the yard.

She turned around, and he heard her hitch in a loud breath.

"Trent, what you are you doing here?"

He sat down beside her and gave her a smile, even though he wanted to kiss her instead. "Visiting you, what else?"

She tilted her head. "I don't know. I thought I told you I didn't want to see you."

He scratched his head. "Did I ever tell you I have a case of selective memory?"

Her lips lifted in amusement. "So you do have flaws?"

"Occasionally. None of us are perfect."

"Have you ever thought about what makes a home, Trent?"

Her question surprised him so that he stared up at the sky, looking for answers. "I used to think it was as simple as a solid foundation." He leveled his glance at her. "Pretty naive, huh?"

"You've got to start somewhere. For me, home was a place to escape from and I used to wonder why I ever came back," she said quietly.

"What changed?" he asked.

She cast him a shy smile. "Just a little sunshine that chased all my clouds away."

"Mother Nature gets all the credit, and it had nothing to do with me?" he joked.

"It had everything to do with you, but I didn't want to admit it until recently."

Trent leaned back against the swing and folded his hands behind his head. "Tonight is your last night in the house?"

Sonya nodded and turned away. "How did you know?"

"I spoke to Nelda. She told me everything. You could have told me what happened, Sonya."

She glanced over at him, fire in her eyes. "You should have known."

He'd expected her anger and he would handle it with care and kindness.

"When I said I don't get involved in the business side, I meant it." He put his hands in his lap and stared straight ahead. "Except when special circumstances arise."

He turned his head slowly, and found that she was staring at him. "And losing your family home meets that requirement."

"What are you trying to say, Trent?"

He took her hand. "Tonight won't be the last night, not if you don't want it to be." He took an envelope out of his jacket pocket. "This will explain everything."

She took it from him, unfolded and read. "You've paid off the mortgage and purchased the home? That's old news."

He held his hands to his chest when she tried to

give it back to him. "Read it a little more carefully, especially the signature. It belongs to me, not my company. I tore up the original contract and negotiated a new one with the bank and your aunt."

She balanced the document on her knees and flipped through it. "I'm looking for what's going to happen to the house. Are you going to tear it down?"

"No. How can I when you and I are going to be living in it as man and wife?"

Tears sprang to her widened eyes, and she covered her mouth with her hands.

"What did you just say?"

Trent got down on one knee, looked into her eyes and cradled her hands in his.

"I love you, Sonya. Will you marry me, and spend your life with me, in this home, forever?"

Her lips began to quiver. "I don't know which question to answer first!"

"I think a single yes will do for both."

He smiled and kissed her knuckles as he drew an engagement ring out of his pocket.

"Will this sweeten the deal?"

He held up six carats of glittery diamonds in a platinum setting. His insides whirled in relief as she threw her arms around his neck and gave him a passionate kiss.

"I love you, Trent."

He slipped the ring on her finger and her squeals of delight were music to his ears. "I wasn't sure I was ever going to see you again, so I didn't want to take a chance that I wouldn't. Plus, I missed bringing you presents."

She held up her hand and admired the ring. "This is the best present you could have ever given me. It's absolutely gorgeous."

Tears rolled down her cheeks, and she looked up at him. "I can't believe you've done all this for me, Trent. Even though it took me so long to tell you I love you, you must have known that I did."

He nodded and cradled her face in his hands. "We're going to have a beautiful life together, Sonya. You never have to worry about losing this house or the land, or me, ever again."

She gave him the sultry smile that had won his heart.

"Now that's a deal I can't resist."

* * * * *

COMING NEXT MONTH
Available September 18, 2018

#589 SEDUCTIVE MEMORY
Moonlight and Passion • by AlTonya Washington
A chance encounter with Paula Starker is all entrepreneur Linus Brooks needs
to try to win back the sultry Philadelphia DA. And where better to romance
her than on a tropical island? But before they can share a future, Linus will
have to reveal his tragic secret...

#590 A LOS ANGELES PASSION
Millionaire Moguls • by Sherelle Green
Award-winning screenwriter Trey Moore agrees to look after his infant
nephew for two weeks. Gorgeous Kiara Woods, owner of LA's glitziest day
care, offers to help. While she's teaching Trey babysitting 101, she's falling
hard for the millionaire. But can she risk revealing a painful truth that's
already cost her so much?

#591 HER PERFECT PLEASURE
Miami Strong • by Lindsay Evans
Lawyer and businessman Carter Diallo solves
problems for his powerful family's corporation.
But when his influential powers fail him, the
Diallos bring in PR wizard—and Carter's
ex-lover—Jade Tremaine. Ten years ago, Carter left
Jade emotionally devastated. Now the guy known
as The Magic Man must win back Jade's trust...

#592 TEMPTING THE BILLIONAIRE
Passion Grove • by Niobia Bryant
Betrayed by his fiancée, self-made billionaire
Chance Castillo plans to sue his ex for her share
of their million-dollar wedding. His unexpected
attraction to his new attorney takes his mind
off his troubles. But Ngozi Johns *never* dates a
client. Until one steamy night with the gorgeous
Dominican changes *everything*.

Get 4 FREE REWARDS!

We'll send you 2 FREE Books plus 2 FREE Mystery Gifts.

Harlequin® Desire books feature heroes who have it all: wealth, status, incredible good looks... everything but the right woman.

FREE Value Over **$20**

SPECIAL EXCERPT FROM

*Award-winning screenwriter Trey Moore agrees to look
after his infant nephew for two weeks, and for once he's
out of his depth. Gorgeous Kiara Woods, owner of
LA's glitziest day care, offers help. While she's teaching
Trey Babysitting 101, she's falling hard for the sexy
millionaire. But can she risk revealing a painful truth
that's already cost her so much?*

Read on for a sneak peek at
A Los Angeles Passion/
*the next exciting installment in the
Millionaire Moguls continuity by Sherelle Green!*

"I had a nice time tonight," Kiara said when she reached the door.
When she didn't hear a response, she turned around to find him watching her intently.

"I had a nice time, as well." Trey took a step closer to her. "I enjoyed
getting to know you a little better." He was so close, Kiara was afraid
to breathe.

"Me, too," she whispered. His eyes dropped to her lips and stayed
there for a while. After a few moments, she forced herself to swallow
the lump in her throat.

He took another step closer, so she took another step back, only to
be met with the door. When his hand reached up to cup her face, Kiara
completely froze. *There's no way he's going to kiss me, right? We just
met each other.*

"Do you want me to stop?" he asked.

Say yes. Say yes. Say yes. "No," she said, moments before his lips
came crashing down onto hers. Her hands flew to the back of his neck
as he gently pushed her against the door. Kiara had experienced plenty

KPEXP0918

of first kisses in the past, but this was unlike any first kiss she'd ever had. Trey's lips were soft, yet demanding. Eager, yet controlled. When she parted her lips to get a better taste, his tongue briefly swooped into her mouth before he ended their kiss with a soft peck and backed away.

Kiara couldn't be sure how she looked, but she certainly felt unhinged and downright aroused.

"Come on," Trey said with a nod. "I'll walk you to your car."

How is he even functioning after that kiss? Kiara felt like she glided to the car, rather than walked. Yet Trey looked as composed as ever.

"We should get together again soon," Trey said, opening her car door. Kiara sat down in the driver's seat and looked up at Trey. He flashed her a sexy smile.

"And for the record, this was definitely a date," Trey said with a wink. "I didn't stop kissing you because I wasn't enjoying it, nor was I trying to tease you. I stopped kissing you because if I hadn't, I'd be ready to drag you into my bedroom. Which also brings me to the reason I didn't show you my bedroom. I didn't trust myself not to make a move." Trey leaned a little closer. "When we make love, I want us to know one another a little better, so I forced myself to stop kissing you tonight and it was damn hard to do so. Have a good night, Kiara."

Trey softly kissed her cheek and closed her door before she could vocalize a response. Quite frankly, she didn't think she had anything to say anyway. Her mind was still reeling and her lips were still tingling from that explosive kiss.

Kiara gave a quick wave. *I told you not to get out of the car earlier*, that voice in her head teased. She started her car and drove away from Trey's house.

"What the hell just happened?" She'd originally thought that she could avoid him or keep their relationship strictly friendly. Now she wasn't so sure. Kissing Trey had awakened desires she thought she'd long buried. Feelings she'd ignored and pushed aside.

Kiara made it to her home a few minutes later. She glanced at her house before dropping her head to the steering wheel. She was in deep and she knew it. To make matters worse, she only lived a five-minute drive from Trey's house, meaning there was no way she was getting any sleep tonight knowing a man that sexy was only a couple miles away.

Don't miss A Los Angeles Passion
*by Sherelle Green, available October 2018
wherever Harlequin® Kimani Romance™
books and ebooks are sold.*

KPEXP0918

*When tech billionaire Benjamin Bennett returns home
for his cousin's wedding, a passionate weekend with his
former crush—his elder sister's best friend
Sloane Sutton—results in two surprises. But can he get
past Sloane's reasons for refusing to marry him
for the twins' sakes?*

*Read on for a sneak peek of
The Billionaire's Legacy by Reese Ryan,
part of the Billionaires and Babies series!*

Benjamin Bennett was a catch by anyone's standards—
even before you factored in his healthy bank account.
But he was her best friend's little brother. And though he
was all grown-up now, he was just a kid compared to her.

Flirting with Benji would start tongues wagging all
over Magnolia Lake. Not that she cared what they thought
of her. But if the whole town started talking, it would
make things uncomfortable for the people she loved.

"Thanks for the dance."

Benji lowered their joined hands but didn't let go.
Instead, he leaned down, his lips brushing her ear and his
well-trimmed beard gently scraping her neck. "Let's get
out of here."

It was a bad idea. A really bad idea.

Her cheeks burned. "But it's your cousin's wedding."

He nodded toward Blake, who was dancing with his

bride, Savannah, as their infant son slept on his shoulder. The man was in complete bliss.

"I doubt he'll notice I'm gone. Besides, you'd be rescuing me. If Jeb Dawson tells me one more time about his latest invention—"

"Okay, okay." Sloane held back a giggle as she glanced around the room. "You need to escape as badly as I do. But there's no way we're leaving here together. It'd be on the front page of the newspaper by morning."

"Valid point." Benji chuckled. "So meet me at the cabin."

"The cabin on the lake?" She had so many great memories of weekends spent there.

It would just be two old friends catching up on each other's lives. Nothing wrong with that.

She repeated it three times in her head. But there was nothing friendly about the sensations that danced along her spine when he'd held her in his arms and pinned her with that piercing gaze.

"Okay. Maybe we can catch up over a cup of coffee or something."

"Or something." The corner of his sensuous mouth curved in a smirk.

A shiver ran through her as she wondered, for the briefest moment, how his lips would taste.

Don't miss
The Billionaire's Legacy *by Reese Ryan,*
part of the Billionaires and Babies *series!*

Available October 2018 wherever
Harlequin® Desire books and ebooks are sold.

www.Harlequin.com

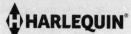